The Haunted Man and the Ghost's Bargin

Charles Dickens

Contents

THE HAUNTED MAN AND THE GHOST'S BARGIN

BY

Charles Dickens

CHAPTER I--The Gift Bestowed

Everybody said so.

Far be it from me to assert that what everybody says must be true. Everybody is, often, as likely to be wrong as right. In the general experience, everybody has been wrong so often, and it has taken, in most instances, such a weary while to find out how wrong, that the authority is proved to be fallible. Everybody may sometimes be right; "but THAT'S no rule," as the ghost of Giles Scroggins says in the ballad.

The dread word, GHOST, recalls me.

Everybody said he looked like a haunted man. The extent of my present claim for everybody is, that they were so far right. He did.

Who could have seen his hollow cheek; his sunken brilliant eye; his black-attired figure, indefinably grim, although well-knit and well-proportioned; his grizzled hair hanging, like tangled sea- weed, about his face,--as if he had been, through his whole life, a lonely mark for the chafing and beating of the great deep of humanity,--but might have said he looked like a haunted man?

Who could have observed his manner, taciturn, thoughtful, gloomy, shadowed by habitual reserve, retiring always and jocund never, with a distraught air of re-verting to a bygone place and time, or of listening to some old echoes in his mind, but might have said it was the manner of a haunted man?

Who could have heard his voice, slow-speaking, deep, and grave, with a natural fulness and melody in it which he seemed to set himself against and stop, but might have said it was the voice of a haunted man?

Who that had seen him in his inner chamber, part library and part laboratory,--for he was, as the world knew, far and wide, a learned man in chemistry, and a teacher on whose lips and hands a crowd of aspiring ears and eyes hung daily,--who that had seen him there, upon a winter night, alone, surrounded by his drugs and instruments and books; the shadow of his shaded lamp a monstrous beetle on the wall, motionless among a crowd of spectral shapes raised there by the flickering of the fire upon the quaint objects around him; some of these phantoms (the reflection of glass vessels that held liquids), trembling at heart like things that knew his power to uncombine them, and to give back their component parts to fire and vapour;-- who that had seen him then, his work done, and he pondering in his chair before the rusted grate and red flame, moving his thin mouth as if in speech, but silent as the dead, would not have said that the man seemed haunted and the chamber too?

Who might not, by a very easy flight of fancy, have believed that everything about him took this haunted tone, and that he lived on haunted ground?

His dwelling was so solitary and vault-like,--an old, retired part of an ancient endowment for students, once a brave edifice, planted in an open place, but now the obsolete whim of forgotten architects; smoke-age-and-weather-darkened, squeezed on every side by the overgrowing of the great city, and choked, like an old well, with stones and bricks; its small quadrangles, lying down in very pits formed by the streets and buildings, which, in course of time, had been constructed above its heavy chimney stalks; its old trees, insulted by the neighbouring smoke, which deigned to droop so low when it was very feeble and the weather very moody; its grass- plots, struggling with the mildewed earth to be grass, or to win any show of compromise; its silent pavements, unaccustomed to the tread of feet, and even to the observation of eyes, except when a stray face looked down from the upper world, wondering what nook it was; its sun-dial in a little bricked-up corner, where no sun had straggled for a hundred years, but where, in compensation for the sun's neglect, the snow would lie for weeks when it lay nowhere else, and the black east wind would spin like a huge humming-top, when in all other places it was silent and still.

His dwelling, at its heart and core--within doors--at his fireside- -was so lowering and old, so crazy, yet so strong, with its worn- eaten beams of wood in the ceiling, and its sturdy floor shelving downward to the great oak chimney-piece; so environed and hemmed in by the pressure of the town yet so remote in fashion, age, and custom; so quiet, yet so thundering with echoes when a distant voice was raised or a door was shut,--echoes, not confined to the many low passages and empty rooms, but rumbling and grumbling till they were stifled in the heavy air of the forgotten Crypt where the Norman arches were half-buried in the earth.

You should have seen him in his dwelling about twilight, in the dead winter time.

When the wind was blowing, shrill and shrewd, with the going down of the blurred sun. When it was just so dark, as that the forms of things were indistinct and big--but not wholly lost. When sitters by the fire began to see wild faces and figures, mountains and abysses, ambuscades and armies, in the coals. When people in the streets bent down their heads and ran before the weather. When those who were obliged to meet it, were stopped at angry corners, stung by wandering snow-flakes alighting on the lashes of their eyes,--which fell too sparingly, and were blown away too quickly, to leave a trace upon the frozen ground. When windows of private houses closed up tight and warm. When lighted gas began to burst forth in the busy and the quiet streets, fast blackening otherwise. When stray pedestrians, shivering along the latter, looked down at the glowing fires in kitchens, and sharpened their sharp appetites by sniffing up the fragrance of whole miles of dinners.

When travellers by land were bitter cold, and looked wearily on gloomy land-scapes, rustling and shuddering in the blast. When mariners at sea, outlying upon icy yards, were tossed and swung above the howling ocean dreadfully. When lighthouses, on rocks and headlands, showed solitary and watchful; and benighted sea-birds breasted on against their ponderous lanterns, and fell dead. When little readers of story-books, by the firelight, trembled to think of Cassim Baba cut into quarters, hanging in the Robbers' Cave, or had some small misgivings that the fierce little old woman, with the crutch, who used to start out of the box in the merchant Abudah's bedroom, might, one of these nights, be found upon the stairs, in the long, cold, dusky journey up to bed.

When, in rustic places, the last glimmering of daylight died away from the ends of avenues; and the trees, arching overhead, were sullen and black. When, in parks and woods, the high wet fern and sodden moss, and beds of fallen leaves, and trunks of trees, were lost to view, in masses of impenetrable shade. When mists arose from dyke, and fen, and river. When lights in old halls and in cottage windows, were a cheerful sight. When the mill stopped, the wheelwright and the blacksmith shut their workshops, the turnpike- gate closed, the plough and harrow were left lonely in the fields, the labourer and team went home, and the striking of the church clock had a deeper sound than at noon, and the churchyard wicket would be swung no more that night.

When twilight everywhere released the shadows, prisoned up all day, that now closed in and gathered like mustering swarms of ghosts. When they stood lowering, in corners of rooms, and frowned out from behind half-opened doors. When they had full possession of unoccupied apartments. When they danced upon the floors, and walls, and ceilings of inhabited chambers, while the fire was low, and withdrew like ebbing waters when it sprang into a blaze. When they fantastically mocked the shapes of household objects, making the nurse an ogress, the rocking-horse a monster, the wondering child, half-scared and half-amused, a stranger to itself,--the very tongs upon the hearth, a straddling giant with his arms a-kimbo, evidently smelling the blood of Englishmen, and wanting to grind people's bones to make his bread.

When these shadows brought into the minds of older people, other thoughts, and showed them different images. When they stole from their retreats, in the like-nesses of forms and faces from the past, from the grave, from the deep, deep gulf, where the things that might have been, and never were, are always wandering.

When he sat, as already mentioned, gazing at the fire. When, as it rose and fell, the shadows went and came. When he took no heed of them, with his bodily eyes; but, let them come or let them go, looked fixedly at the fire. You should have seen him, then.

When the sounds that had arisen with the shadows, and come out of their lurking-places at the twilight summons, seemed to make a deeper stillness all about him. When the wind was rumbling in the chimney, and sometimes crooning, sometimes howling, in the house. When the old trees outside were so shaken and beaten, that one querulous old rook, unable to sleep, protested now and then, in a feeble, dozy, high-up "Caw!" When, at intervals, the window trembled, the rusty vane upon the turret-top complained, the clock beneath it recorded that another quarter of an hour was gone, or the fire collapsed and fell in with a rattle.

- When a knock came at his door, in short, as he was sitting so, and roused him.

"Who's that?" said he. "Come in!"

Surely there had been no figure leaning on the back of his chair; no face looking over it. It is certain that no gliding footstep touched the floor, as he lifted up his head, with a start, and spoke. And yet there was no mirror in the room on whose surface his own form could have cast its shadow for a moment; and, Something had passed darkly and gone!

"I'm humbly fearful, sir," said a fresh-coloured busy man, holding the door open with his foot for the admission of himself and a wooden tray he carried, and letting it go again by very gentle and careful degrees, when he and the tray had got in, lest it should close noisily, "that it's a good bit past the time to-night. But Mrs. William has been taken off her legs so often" -

"By the wind? Ay! I have heard it rising."

"--By the wind, sir--that it's a mercy she got home at all. Oh dear, yes. Yes. It was by the wind, Mr. Redlaw. By the wind."

He had, by this time, put down the tray for dinner, and was employed in lighting the lamp, and spreading a cloth on the table. From this employment he desisted in a hurry, to stir and feed the fire, and then resumed it; the lamp he had lighted, and the blaze that rose under his hand, so quickly changing the appearance of the room, that it seemed as if the mere coming in of his fresh red face and active manner had made the pleasant alteration.

"Mrs. William is of course subject at any time, sir, to be taken off her balance by the elements. She is not formed superior to THAT."

"No," returned Mr. Redlaw good-naturedly, though abruptly.

"No, sir. Mrs. William may be taken off her balance by Earth; as for example, last Sunday week, when sloppy and greasy, and she going out to tea with her newest sister-in-law, and having a pride in herself, and wishing to appear perfectly spotless though pedestrian. Mrs. William may be taken off her balance by Air; as being once over-persuaded by a friend to try a swing at Peckham Fair, which acted on her constitution instantly like a steam-boat. Mrs. William may be taken off her balance by Fire; as on a false alarm of engines at her mother's, when she went two miles in her nightcap. Mrs. William may be taken off her balance by Water; as at Battersea, when rowed into the piers by her young nephew, Charley Swidger junior, aged twelve, which had no idea of boats whatever. But these are elements. Mrs. William must be taken out of elements for the strength of HER character to come into play."

As he stopped for a reply, the reply was "Yes," in the same tone as before.

"Yes, sir. Oh dear, yes!" said Mr. Swidger, still proceeding with his preparations, and checking them off as he made them. "That's where it is, sir. That's what I always say myself, sir. Such a many of us Swidgers!--Pepper. Why there's my father, sir, superannuated keeper and custodian of this Institution, eighty- seven year old. He's a Swidger!--Spoon."

"True, William," was the patient and abstracted answer, when he stopped again.

"Yes, sir," said Mr. Swidger. "That's what I always say, sir. You may call him the trunk of the tree!--Bread. Then you come to his successor, my unworthy self--Salt--and Mrs. William, Swidgers both.--Knife and fork. Then you come to all my brothers and their families, Swidgers, man and woman, boy and girl. Why, what with cousins, uncles, aunts, and relationships of this, that, and t'other degree, and whatnot degree, and marriages, and lyings-in, the Swidgers--Tumbler--might take hold of hands, and make a ring round England!"

Receiving no reply at all here, from the thoughtful man whom he addressed, Mr. William approached, him nearer, and made a feint of accidentally knocking the table with a decanter, to rouse him. The moment he succeeded, he went on, as if in great alacrity of acquiescence.

"Yes, sir! That's just what I say myself, sir. Mrs. William and me have often said so. 'There's Swidgers enough,' we say, 'without OUR voluntary contributions,'--Butter. In fact, sir, my father is a family in himself--Castors--to take care of; and it happens all for the best that we have no child of our own, though it's made Mrs. William rather quiet-like, too. Quite ready for the fowl and mashed potatoes, sir? Mrs. William said she'd dish in ten minutes when I left the Lodge."

"I am quite ready," said the other, waking as from a dream, and walking slowly to and fro.

"Mrs. William has been at it again, sir!" said the keeper, as he stood warming a plate at the fire, and pleasantly shading his face with it. Mr. Redlaw stopped in his walking, and an expression of interest appeared in him.

"What I always say myself, sir. She WILL do it! There's a motherly feeling in Mrs. William's breast that must and will have went."

"What has she done?"

"Why, sir, not satisfied with being a sort of mother to all the young gentlemen that come up from a variety of parts, to attend your courses of lectures at this ancient foundation--its surprising how stone-chaney catches the heat this frosty weather, to be sure!" Here he turned the plate, and cooled his fingers.

"Well?" said Mr. Redlaw.

"That's just what I say myself, sir," returned Mr. William, speaking over his shoulder, as if in ready and delighted assent. "That's exactly where it is, sir! There ain't one of our students but appears to regard Mrs. William in that light. Every day, right through the course, they puts their heads into the Lodge, one after another, and have all got something to tell her, or something to ask her. 'Swidge' is the appellation by which they speak of Mrs. William in general, among themselves, I'm told; but that's what I say, sir. Better be called ever so far out of your name, if it's done in real liking, than have it made ever so much of, and not cared about! What's a name for? To know a person by. If Mrs. William is known by something better than her name--I allude to Mrs. William's qualities and disposition--never mind her name, though it IS Swidger, by rights. Let 'em call her Swidge, Widge, Bridge--Lord! London Bridge, Blackfriars, Chelsea, Putney, Waterloo, or Hammersmith Suspension--if they like."

The close of this triumphant oration brought him and the plate to the table, upon which he half laid and half dropped it, with a lively sense of its being thoroughly heated, just as the subject of his praises entered the room, bearing another tray and a lantern, and followed by a venerable old man with long grey hair.

Mrs. William, like Mr. William, was a simple, innocent-looking person, in whose smooth cheeks the cheerful red of her husband's official waistcoat was very pleasantly repeated. But whereas Mr. William's light hair stood on end all over his head, and seemed to draw his eyes up with it in an excess of bustling readiness for anything, the dark brown hair of Mrs. William was carefully smoothed down, and waved away under a trim tidy cap, in the most exact and quiet manner imaginable. Whereas Mr. William's very trousers hitched themselves up at the ankles, as if it were not in their iron-grey nature to rest without looking about them, Mrs. William's neatly-flowered skirts--red and white, like her own pretty face--were as composed and orderly, as if the very wind that blew so hard out of doors could not disturb one of their folds. Whereas his coat had something of a fly-away and half-off appearance about the collar and breast, her little bodice was so placid and neat, that there should have been protection for her, in it, had she needed any, with the roughest people. Who could have had the heart to make so calm a bosom swell with grief, or throb with fear, or flutter with a thought of shame! To whom would its repose and peace have not appealed against disturbance, like the innocent slumber of a child!

"Punctual, of course, Milly," said her husband, relieving her of the tray, "or it wouldn't be you. Here's Mrs. William, sir!--He looks lonelier than ever to-night," whispering to his wife, as he was taking the tray, "and ghostlier altogether."

Without any show of hurry or noise, or any show of herself even, she was so calm and quiet, Milly set the dishes she had brought upon the table,--Mr. William, after much clattering and running about, having only gained possession of a butter-boat of gravy, which he stood ready to serve.

"What is that the old man has in his arms?" asked Mr. Redlaw, as he sat down to his solitary meal.

"Holly, sir," replied the quiet voice of Milly.

"That's what I say myself, sir," interposed Mr. William, striking in with the butter-boat. "Berries is so seasonable to the time of year!--Brown gravy!"

"Another Christmas come, another year gone!" murmured the Chemist, with a gloomy sigh. "More figures in the lengthening sum of recollection that we work and work at to our torment, till Death idly jumbles all together, and rubs all out. So, Philip!" breaking off, and raising his voice as he addressed the old man, standing apart, with his glistening burden in his arms, from which the quiet Mrs. William took small branches, which she noiselessly trimmed with her scissors, and decorated the room with, while her aged father-in-law looked on much interested in the ceremony.

"My duty to you, sir," returned the old man. "Should have spoke before, sir, but know your ways, Mr. Redlaw--proud to say--and wait till spoke to! Merry Christmas, sir, and Happy New Year, and many of 'em. Have had a pretty many of 'em myself--ha, ha!--and may take the liberty of wishing 'em. I'm eighty-seven!"

"Have you had so many that were merry and happy?" asked the other.

"Ay, sir, ever so many," returned the old man.

"Is his memory impaired with age? It is to be expected now," said Mr. Redlaw, turning to the son, and speaking lower.

"Not a morsel of it, sir," replied Mr. William. "That's exactly what I say myself, sir. There never was such a memory as my father's. He's the most wonderful man in the world. He don't know what forgetting means. It's the very observation I'm always making to Mrs. William, sir, if you'll believe me!"

Mr. Swidger, in his polite desire to seem to acquiesce at all events, delivered this as if there were no iota of contradiction in it, and it were all said in unbounded and unqualified assent.

The Chemist pushed his plate away, and, rising from the table, walked across the room to where the old man stood looking at a little sprig of holly in his hand.

"It recalls the time when many of those years were old and new, then?" he said, observing him attentively, and touching him on the shoulder. "Does it?"

"Oh many, many!" said Philip, half awaking from his reverie. "I'm eighty-seven!"

"Merry and happy, was it?" asked the Chemist in a low voice. "Merry and happy, old man?"

"Maybe as high as that, no higher," said the old man, holding out his hand a little way above the level of his knee, and looking retrospectively at his questioner, "when I first remember 'em! Cold, sunshiny day it was, out a-walking, when some one--it was my mother as sure as you stand there, though I don't know what her blessed face was like, for she took ill and died that Christmas- time--told me they were food for birds. The pretty little fellow thought--that's me, you understand-- that birds' eyes were so bright, perhaps, because the berries that they lived on in the winter were so bright. I recollect that. And I'm eighty-seven!"

"Merry and happy!" mused the other, bending his dark eyes upon the stooping figure, with a smile of compassion. "Merry and happy--and remember well?"

"Ay, ay, ay!" resumed the old man, catching the last words. "I remember 'em well in my school time, year after year, and all the merry-making that used to come along with them. I was a strong chap then, Mr. Redlaw; and, if you'll believe me, hadn't my match at football within ten mile. Where's my son William? Hadn't my match at football, William, within ten mile!"

"That's what I always say, father!" returned the son promptly, and with great respect. "You ARE a Swidger, if ever there was one of the family!"

"Dear!" said the old man, shaking his head as he again looked at the holly. "His mother--my son William's my youngest son--and I, have sat among 'em all, boys and girls, little children and babies, many a year, when the berries like these were not shining half so bright all round us, as their bright faces. Many of 'em are gone; she's gone; and my son George (our eldest, who was her pride more than all the rest!) is fallen very low: but I can see them, when I look here, alive and healthy, as they used to be in those days; and I can see him, thank God, in his innocence. It's a blessed thing to me, at eighty-seven."

The keen look that had been fixed upon him with so much earnestness, had gradually sought the ground.

"When my circumstances got to be not so good as formerly, through not being honestly dealt by, and I first come here to be custodian," said the old man, "--which was upwards of fifty years ago--where's my son William? More than half a century ago, William!"

"That's what I say, father," replied the son, as promptly and dutifully as before, "that's exactly where it is. Two times ought's an ought, and twice five ten, and there's a hundred of 'em."

"It was quite a pleasure to know that one of our founders--or more correctly speaking," said the old man, with a great glory in his subject and his knowledge of it, "one of the learned gentlemen that helped endow us in Queen Elizabeth's time, for we were founded afore her day--left in his will, among the other bequests he made us, so much to buy holly, for garnishing the walls and windows, come Christmas. There was something homely and friendly in it. Being but strange here, then, and coming at Christmas time, we took a liking for his very picter that hangs in what used to be, anciently, afore our ten poor gentlemen commuted for an annual stipend in money, our great Dinner Hall.--A sedate gentleman in a peaked beard, with a ruff round his neck, and a scroll below him, in old English letters, 'Lord! keep my memory green!' You know all about him, Mr. Redlaw?"

"I know the portrait hangs there, Philip."

"Yes, sure, it's the second on the right, above the panelling. I was going to say--he has helped to keep MY memory green, I thank him; for going round the building every year, as I'm a doing now, and freshening up the bare rooms with these branches and berries, freshens up my bare old brain. One year brings back another, and that year another, and those others numbers! At last, it seems to me as if the birth-time of our Lord was the birth-time of all I have ever had affection for, or mourned for, or delighted in,--and they're a pretty many, for I'm eighty-seven!"

"Merry and happy," murmured Redlaw to himself.

The room began to darken strangely.

"So you see, sir," pursued old Philip, whose hale wintry cheek had warmed into a ruddier glow, and whose blue eyes had brightened while he spoke, "I have plenty to keep, when I keep this present season. Now, where's my quiet Mouse? Chattering's the sin of my time of life, and there's half the building to do yet, if the cold don't freeze us first, or the wind don't blow us away, or the darkness don't swallow us up."

The quiet Mouse had brought her calm face to his side, and silently taken his arm, before he finished speaking.

"Come away, my dear," said the old man. "Mr. Redlaw won't settle to his dinner, otherwise, till it's cold as the winter. I hope you'll excuse me rambling on, sir, and I wish you good night, and, once again, a merry--"

"Stay!" said Mr. Redlaw, resuming his place at the table, more, it would have seemed from his manner, to reassure the old keeper, than in any remembrance of his own appetite. "Spare me another moment, Philip. William, you were going to tell me something to your excellent wife's honour. It will not be disagreeable to her to hear you praise her. What was it?"

"Why, that's where it is, you see, sir," returned Mr. William Swidger, looking towards his wife in considerable embarrassment. "Mrs. William's got her eye upon me."

"But you're not afraid of Mrs. William's eye?"

"Why, no, sir," returned Mr. Swidger, "that's what I say myself. It wasn't made to be afraid of. It wouldn't have been made so mild, if that was the intention. But I wouldn't like to--Milly!-- him, you know. Down in the Buildings."

Mr. William, standing behind the table, and rummaging disconcertedly among the objects upon it, directed persuasive glances at Mrs. William, and secret jerks of his head and thumb at Mr. Redlaw, as alluring her towards him.

"Him, you know, my love," said Mr. William. "Down in the Buildings. Tell, my dear! You're the works of Shakespeare in comparison with myself. Down in the Buildings, you know, my love.- -Student."

"Student?" repeated Mr. Redlaw, raising his head.

"That's what I say, sir!" cried Mr. William, in the utmost animation of assent. "If it wasn't the poor student down in the Buildings, why should you wish to hear it from Mrs. William's lips? Mrs. William, my dear--Buildings."

"I didn't know," said Milly, with a quiet frankness, free from any haste or confusion, "that William had said anything about it, or I wouldn't have come. I asked him not to. It's a sick young gentleman, sir--and very poor, I am afraid--who is too ill to go home this holiday-time, and lives, unknown to any one, in but a common kind of lodging for a gentleman, down in Jerusalem Buildings. That's all, sir."

"Why have I never heard of him?" said the Chemist, rising hurriedly. "Why has he not made his situation known to me? Sick!- -give me my hat and cloak. Poor!--what house?--what number?"

"Oh, you mustn't go there, sir," said Milly, leaving her father-in- law, and calmly confronting him with her collected little face and folded hands.

"Not go there?"

"Oh dear, no!" said Milly, shaking her head as at a most manifest and self-evident impossibility. "It couldn't be thought of!"

"What do you mean? Why not?"

"Why, you see, sir," said Mr. William Swidger, persuasively and confidentially, "that's what I say. Depend upon it, the young gentleman would never have made his situation known to one of his own sex. Mrs. Williams has got into his confidence, but that's quite different. They all confide in Mrs. William; they all trust HER. A man, sir, couldn't have got a whisper out of him; but woman, sir, and Mrs. William combined--!"

"There is good sense and delicacy in what you say, William," returned Mr. Redlaw, observant of the gentle and composed face at his shoulder. And laying his finger on his lip, he secretly put his purse into her hand.

"Oh dear no, sir!" cried Milly, giving it back again. "Worse and worse! Couldn't be dreamed of!"

Such a staid matter-of-fact housewife she was, and so unruffled by the momentary haste of this rejection, that, an instant afterwards, she was tidily picking up a few leaves which had strayed from between her scissors and her apron, when she had arranged the holly.

Finding, when she rose from her stooping posture, that Mr. Redlaw was still regarding her with doubt and astonishment, she quietly repeated--looking about, the while, for any other fragments that might have escaped her observation:

"Oh dear no, sir! He said that of all the world he would not be known to you, or receive help from you--though he is a student in your class. I have made no terms of secrecy with you, but I trust to your honour completely."

"Why did he say so?"

"Indeed I can't tell, sir," said Milly, after thinking a little, "because I am not at all clever, you know; and I wanted to be useful to him in making things neat and comfortable about him, and employed myself that way. But I know he is poor, and lonely, and I think he is somehow neglected too.--How dark it is!"

The room had darkened more and more. There was a very heavy gloom and shadow gathering behind the Chemist's chair.

"What more about him?" he asked.

"He is engaged to be married when he can afford it," said Milly, "and is study-ing, I think, to qualify himself to earn a living. I have seen, a long time, that he has studied hard and denied himself much.--How very dark it is!"

"It's turned colder, too," said the old man, rubbing his hands. "There's a chill and dismal feeling in the room. Where's my son William? William, my boy, turn the lamp, and rouse the fire!"

Milly's voice resumed, like quiet music very softly played:

"He muttered in his broken sleep yesterday afternoon, after talking to me" (this was to herself) "about some one dead, and some great wrong done that could never be forgotten; but whether to him or to another person, I don't know. Not BY him, I am sure."

"And, in short, Mrs. William, you see--which she wouldn't say herself, Mr. Redlaw, if she was to stop here till the new year after this next one--" said Mr. Wil-liam, coming up to him to speak in his ear, "has done him worlds of good! Bless you, worlds of good! All at home just the same as ever--my father made as snug and comfortable--not a crumb of litter to be found in the house, if you were to offer fifty pound ready money for it--Mrs. William apparently never out of the way--yet

Mrs. William backwards and forwards, backwards and forwards, up and down, up and down, a mother to him!"

The room turned darker and colder, and the gloom and shadow gathering behind the chair was heavier.

"Not content with this, sir, Mrs. William goes and finds, this very night, when she was coming home (why it's not above a couple of hours ago), a creature more like a young wild beast than a young child, shivering upon a door-step. What does Mrs. William do, but brings it home to dry it, and feed it, and keep it till our old Bounty of food and flannel is given away, on Christmas morning! If it ever felt a fire before, it's as much as ever it did; for it's sitting in the old Lodge chimney, staring at ours as if its ravenous eyes would never shut again. It's sitting there, at least," said Mr. William, correcting himself, on reflection, "unless it's bolted!"

"Heaven keep her happy!" said the Chemist aloud, "and you too, Philip! and you, William! I must consider what to do in this. I may desire to see this student, I'll not detain you any longer now. Good-night!"

"I thank'ee, sir, I thank'ee!" said the old man, "for Mouse, and for my son William, and for myself. Where's my son William? William, you take the lantern and go on first, through them long dark passages, as you did last year and the year afore. Ha ha! *I* remember--though I'm eighty-seven! 'Lord, keep my memory green!' It's a very good prayer, Mr. Redlaw, that of the learned gentleman in the peaked beard, with a ruff round his neck--hangs up, second on the right above the panelling, in what used to be, afore our ten poor gentlemen commuted, our great Dinner Hall. 'Lord, keep my memory green!' It's very good and pious, sir. Amen! Amen!"

As they passed out and shut the heavy door, which, however carefully withheld, fired a long train of thundering reverberations when it shut at last, the room turned darker.

As he fell a musing in his chair alone, the healthy holly withered on the wall, and dropped--dead branches.

As the gloom and shadow thickened behind him, in that place where it had been gathering so darkly, it took, by slow degrees,--or out of it there came, by some unreal, unsubstantial process--not to be traced by any human sense,--an awful likeness of himself!

Ghastly and cold, colourless in its leaden face and hands, but with his features, and his bright eyes, and his grizzled hair, and dressed in the gloomy shadow of his dress, it came into his terrible appearance of existence, motionless, without a sound. As HE leaned his arm upon the elbow of his chair, ruminating before the fire, IT leaned upon the chair-back, close above him, with its appalling copy of his face looking where his face looked, and bearing the expression his face bore.

This, then, was the Something that had passed and gone already. This was the dread companion of the haunted man!

It took, for some moments, no more apparent heed of him, than he of it. The Christmas Waits were playing somewhere in the distance, and, through his thoughtfulness, he seemed to listen to the music. It seemed to listen too.

At length he spoke; without moving or lifting up his face.

"Here again!" he said.

"Here again," replied the Phantom.

"I see you in the fire," said the haunted man; "I hear you in music, in the wind, in the dead stillness of the night."

The Phantom moved its head, assenting.

"Why do you come, to haunt me thus?"

"I come as I am called," replied the Ghost.

"No. Unbidden," exclaimed the Chemist.

"Unbidden be it," said the Spectre. "It is enough. I am here."

Hitherto the light of the fire had shone on the two faces--if the dread lineaments behind the chair might be called a face--both addressed towards it, as at first, and neither looking at the other. But, now, the haunted man turned, suddenly, and stared upon the Ghost. The Ghost, as sudden in its motion, passed to before the chair, and stared on him.

The living man, and the animated image of himself dead, might so have looked, the one upon the other. An awful survey, in a lonely and remote part of an empty old pile of building, on a winter night, with the loud wind going by upon its journey of mystery-- whence or whither, no man knowing since the world began--and the stars, in unimaginable millions, glittering through it, from eternal space, where the world's bulk is as a grain, and its hoary age is infancy.

"Look upon me!" said the Spectre. "I am he, neglected in my youth, and miserably poor, who strove and suffered, and still strove and suffered, until I hewed out knowledge from the mine where it was buried, and made rugged steps thereof, for my worn feet to rest and rise on."

"I AM that man," returned the Chemist.

"No mother's self-denying love," pursued the Phantom, "no father's counsel, aided ME. A stranger came into my father's place when I was but a child, and I was easily an alien from my mother's heart. My parents, at the best, were of that sort whose care soon ends, and whose duty is soon done; who cast their offspring loose, early, as birds do theirs; and, if they do well, claim the merit; and, if ill, the pity."

It paused, and seemed to tempt and goad him with its look, and with the manner of its speech, and with its smile.

"I am he," pursued the Phantom, "who, in this struggle upward, found a friend. I made him--won him--bound him to me! We worked together, side by side. All the love and confidence that in my earlier youth had had no outlet, and found no expression, I bestowed on him."

"Not all," said Redlaw, hoarsely.

"No, not all," returned the Phantom. "I had a sister."

The haunted man, with his head resting on his hands, replied "I had!" The Phantom, with an evil smile, drew closer to the chair, and resting its chin upon its folded hands, its folded hands upon the back, and looking down into his face with searching eyes, that seemed instinct with fire, went on:

"Such glimpses of the light of home as I had ever known, had streamed from her. How young she was, how fair, how loving! I took her to the first poor roof that I was master of, and made it rich. She came into the darkness of my life, and made it bright.-- She is before me!"

"I saw her, in the fire, but now. I hear her in music, in the wind, in the dead stillness of the night," returned the haunted man.

"DID he love her?" said the Phantom, echoing his contemplative tone. "I think he did, once. I am sure he did. Better had she loved him less--less secretly, less dearly, from the shallower depths of a more divided heart!"

"Let me forget it!" said the Chemist, with an angry motion of his hand. "Let me blot it from my memory!"

The Spectre, without stirring, and with its unwinking, cruel eyes still fixed upon his face, went on:

"A dream, like hers, stole upon my own life."

"It did," said Redlaw.

"A love, as like hers," pursued the Phantom, "as my inferior nature might cherish, arose in my own heart. I was too poor to bind its object to my fortune then, by any thread of promise or entreaty. I loved her far too well, to seek to do it. But, more than ever I had striven in my life, I strove to climb! Only an inch gained, brought me something nearer to the height. I toiled up! In the late pauses of my labour at that time,--my sister (sweet companion!) still sharing with me the expiring embers and the cooling hearth,--when day was breaking, what pictures of the future did I see!"

"I saw them, in the fire, but now," he murmured. "They come back to me in music, in the wind, in the dead stillness of the night, in the revolving years."

"--Pictures of my own domestic life, in aftertime, with her who was the inspiration of my toil. Pictures of my sister, made the wife of my dear friend, on equal terms--for he had some inheritance, we none--pictures of our sobered age and mellowed happiness, and of the golden links, extending back so far, that should bind us, and our children, in a radiant garland," said the Phantom.

"Pictures," said the haunted man, "that were delusions. Why is it my doom to remember them too well!"

"Delusions," echoed the Phantom in its changeless voice, and glaring on him with its changeless eyes. "For my friend (in whose breast my confidence was locked as in my own), passing between me and the centre of the system of my hopes and struggles, won her to himself, and shattered my frail universe. My sister, doubly dear, doubly devoted, doubly cheerful in my home, lived on to see me famous, and my old ambition so rewarded when its spring was broken, and then--"

"Then died," he interposed. "Died, gentle as ever; happy; and with no concern but for her brother. Peace!"

The Phantom watched him silently.

"Remembered!" said the haunted man, after a pause. "Yes. So well remembered, that even now, when years have passed, and nothing is more idle or more visionary to me than the boyish love so long outlived, I think of it with sympathy, as if it were a younger brother's or a son's. Sometimes I even wonder when her heart first inclined to him, and how it had been affected towards me.--Not lightly, once, I think.--But that is nothing. Early unhappiness, a wound from a hand I loved and trusted, and a loss that nothing can replace, outlive such fancies."

"Thus," said the Phantom, "I bear within me a Sorrow and a Wrong. Thus I prey upon myself. Thus, memory is my curse; and, if I could forget my sorrow and my wrong, I would!"

"Mocker!" said the Chemist, leaping up, and making, with a wrathful hand, at the throat of his other self. "Why have I always that taunt in my ears?"

"Forbear!" exclaimed the Spectre in an awful voice. "Lay a hand on Me, and die!"

He stopped midway, as if its words had paralysed him, and stood looking on it. It had glided from him; it had its arm raised high in warning; and a smile passed over its unearthly features, as it reared its dark figure in triumph.

"If I could forget my sorrow and wrong, I would," the Ghost repeated. "If I could forget my sorrow and my wrong, I would!"

"Evil spirit of myself," returned the haunted man, in a low, trembling tone, "my life is darkened by that incessant whisper."

"It is an echo," said the Phantom.

"If it be an echo of my thoughts--as now, indeed, I know it is," rejoined the haunted man, "why should I, therefore, be tormented? It is not a selfish thought. I suffer it to range beyond myself. All men and women have their sorrows,--most of them their wrongs; ingratitude, and sordid jealousy, and interest, besetting all degrees of life. Who would not forget their sorrows and their wrongs?"

"Who would not, truly, and be happier and better for it?" said the Phantom.

"These revolutions of years, which we commemorate," proceeded Redlaw, "what do THEY recall! Are there any minds in which they do not re-awaken some sorrow, or some trouble? What is the remembrance of the old man who was here to-night? A tissue of sorrow and trouble."

"But common natures," said the Phantom, with its evil smile upon its glassy face, "unenlightened minds and ordinary spirits, do not feel or reason on these things like men of higher cultivation and profounder thought."

"Tempter," answered Redlaw, "whose hollow look and voice I dread more than words can express, and from whom some dim foreshadowing of greater fear is stealing over me while I speak, I hear again an echo of my own mind."

"Receive it as a proof that I am powerful," returned the Ghost. "Hear what I offer! Forget the sorrow, wrong, and trouble you have known!"

"Forget them!" he repeated.

"I have the power to cancel their remembrance--to leave but very faint, confused traces of them, that will die out soon," returned the Spectre. "Say! Is it done?"

"Stay!" cried the haunted man, arresting by a terrified gesture the uplifted hand. "I tremble with distrust and doubt of you; and the dim fear you cast upon me deepens into a nameless horror I can hardly bear.--I would not deprive myself of any kindly recollection, or any sympathy that is good for me, or others. What shall I lose, if I assent to this? What else will pass from my remembrance?"

"No knowledge; no result of study; nothing but the intertwisted chain of feelings and associations, each in its turn dependent on, and nourished by, the banished recollections. Those will go."

"Are they so many?" said the haunted man, reflecting in alarm.

"They have been wont to show themselves in the fire, in music, in the wind, in the dead stillness of the night, in the revolving years," returned the Phantom scornfully.

"In nothing else?"

The Phantom held its peace.

But having stood before him, silent, for a little while, it moved towards the fire; then stopped.

"Decide!" it said, "before the opportunity is lost!"

"A moment! I call Heaven to witness," said the agitated man, "that I have never been a hater of any kind,--never morose, indifferent, or hard, to anything around me. If, living here alone, I have made too much of all that was and might have been, and too little of what is, the evil, I believe, has fallen on me, and not on others. But, if there were poison in my body, should I not, possessed of antidotes and knowledge how to use them, use them? If there be poison in my mind, and through this fearful shadow I can cast it out, shall I not cast it out?"

"Say," said the Spectre, "is it done?"

"A moment longer!" he answered hurriedly. "I WOULD FORGET IT IF I COULD! Have *I* thought that, alone, or has it been the thought of thousands upon thousands, generation after generation? All human memory is fraught with sorrow and trouble. My memory is as the memory of other men, but other men have not this choice. Yes, I close the bargain. Yes! I WILL forget my sorrow, wrong, and trouble!"

"Say," said the Spectre, "is it done?"

"It is!"

"IT IS. And take this with you, man whom I here renounce! The gift that I have given, you shall give again, go where you will. Without recovering yourself the power that you have yielded up, you shall henceforth destroy its like in all whom you approach. Your wisdom has discovered that the memory of sorrow, wrong, and trouble is the lot of all mankind, and that mankind would be the happier, in its other memories, without it. Go! Be its benefactor! Freed from such remembrance, from this hour, carry involuntarily the blessing of such freedom with you. Its diffusion is inseparable and inalienable from you. Go! Be happy in the good you have won, and in the good you do!"

The Phantom, which had held its bloodless hand above him while it spoke, as if in some unholy invocation, or some ban; and which had gradually advanced its eyes so close to his, that he could see how they did not participate in the terrible smile upon its face, but were a fixed, unalterable, steady horror melted before him and was gone.

As he stood rooted to the spot, possessed by fear and wonder, and imagining he heard repeated in melancholy echoes, dying away fainter and fainter, the words, "Destroy its like in all whom you approach!" a shrill cry reached his ears. It came, not from the passages beyond the door, but from another part of the old building, and sounded like the cry of some one in the dark who had lost the way.

He looked confusedly upon his hands and limbs, as if to be assured of his identity, and then shouted in reply, loudly and wildly; for there was a strangeness and terror upon him, as if he too were lost.

The cry responding, and being nearer, he caught up the lamp, and raised a heavy curtain in the wall, by which he was accustomed to pass into and out of the theatre where he lectured,--which adjoined his room. Associated with youth and animation, and a high amphitheatre of faces which his entrance charmed to interest in a moment, it was a ghostly place when all this life was faded out of it, and stared upon him like an emblem of Death.

"Halloa!" he cried. "Halloa! This way! Come to the light!" When, as he held the curtain with one hand, and with the other raised the lamp and tried to pierce the gloom that filled the place, something rushed past him into the room like a wild-cat, and crouched down in a corner.

"What is it?" he said, hastily.

He might have asked "What is it?" even had he seen it well, as presently he did when he stood looking at it gathered up in its corner.

A bundle of tatters, held together by a hand, in size and form almost an infant's, but in its greedy, desperate little clutch, a bad old man's. A face rounded and smoothed by some half-dozen years, but pinched and twisted by the experiences of a life. Bright eyes, but not youthful. Naked feet, beautiful in their childish delicacy,--ugly in the blood and dirt that cracked upon them. A baby savage, a young monster, a child who had never been a child, a creature who might live to take the outward form of man, but who, within, would live and perish a mere beast.

Used, already, to be worried and hunted like a beast, the boy crouched down as he was looked at, and looked back again, and interposed his arm to ward off the expected blow.

"I'll bite," he said, "if you hit me!"

The time had been, and not many minutes since, when such a sight as this would have wrung the Chemist's heart. He looked upon it now, coldly; but with a heavy effort to remember something--he did not know what--he asked the boy what he did there, and whence he came.

"Where's the woman?" he replied. "I want to find the woman."

"Who?"

"The woman. Her that brought me here, and set me by the large fire. She was so long gone, that I went to look for her, and lost myself. I don't want you. I want the woman."

He made a spring, so suddenly, to get away, that the dull sound of his naked feet upon the floor was near the curtain, when Redlaw caught him by his rags.

"Come! you let me go!" muttered the boy, struggling, and clenching his teeth. "I've done nothing to you. Let me go, will you, to the woman!"

"That is not the way. There is a nearer one," said Redlaw, detaining him, in the same blank effort to remember some association that ought, of right, to bear upon this monstrous object. "What is your name?"

"Got none."

"Where do you live?

"Live! What's that?"

The boy shook his hair from his eyes to look at him for a moment, and then, twisting round his legs and wrestling with him, broke again into his repetition of "You let me go, will you? I want to find the woman."

The Chemist led him to the door. "This way," he said, looking at him still confusedly, but with repugnance and avoidance, growing out of his coldness. "I'll take you to her."

The sharp eyes in the child's head, wandering round the room, lighted on the table where the remnants of the dinner were.

"Give me some of that!" he said, covetously.

"Has she not fed you?"

"I shall be hungry again to-morrow, sha'n't I? Ain't I hungry every day?"

Finding himself released, he bounded at the table like some small animal of prey, and hugging to his breast bread and meat, and his own rags, all together, said:

"There! Now take me to the woman!"

As the Chemist, with a new-born dislike to touch him, sternly motioned him to follow, and was going out of the door, he trembled and stopped.

"The gift that I have given, you shall give again, go where you will!"

The Phantom's words were blowing in the wind, and the wind blew chill upon him.

"I'll not go there, to-night," he murmured faintly. "I'll go nowhere to-night.

Boy! straight down this long-arched passage, and past the great dark door into the yard,--you see the fire shining on the window there."

"The woman's fire?" inquired the boy.

He nodded, and the naked feet had sprung away. He came back with his lamp, locked his door hastily, and sat down in his chair, covering his face like one who was frightened at himself.

For now he was, indeed, alone. Alone, alone.

CHAPTER II--The Gift Diffused

A small man sat in a small parlour, partitioned off from a small shop by a small screen, pasted all over with small scraps of newspapers. In company with the small man, was almost any amount of small children you may please to name--at least it seemed so; they made, in that very limited sphere of action, such an imposing effect, in point of numbers.

Of these small fry, two had, by some strong machinery, been got into bed in a corner, where they might have reposed snugly enough in the sleep of innocence, but for a constitutional propensity to keep awake, and also to scuffle in and out of bed. The immediate occasion of these predatory dashes at the waking world, was the construction of an oyster-shell wall in a corner, by two other youths of tender age; on which fortification the two in bed made harassing descents (like those accursed Picts and Scots who beleaguer the early historical studies of most young Britons), and then withdrew to their own territory.

In addition to the stir attendant on these inroads, and the retorts of the invaded, who pursued hotly, and made lunges at the bed- clothes under which the marauders took refuge, another little boy, in another little bed, contributed his mite of confusion to the family stock, by casting his boots upon the waters; in other words, by launching these and several small objects, inoffensive in themselves, though of a hard substance considered as missiles, at the disturbers of his repose,--who were not slow to return these compliments.

Besides which, another little boy--the biggest there, but still little--was tottering to and fro, bent on one side, and considerably affected in his knees by the weight of a large baby, which he was supposed by a fiction that obtains sometimes in sanguine families, to be hushing to sleep. But oh! the inexhaustible regions of contemplation and watchfulness into which this baby's eyes were then only beginning to compose themselves to stare, over his unconscious shoulder!

It was a very Moloch of a baby, on whose insatiate altar the whole existence of this particular young brother was offered up a daily sacrifice. Its personality may be said to have consisted in its never being quiet, in any one place, for five consecutive minutes, and never going to sleep when required. "Tetterby's baby" was as well known in the neighbourhood as the postman or the pot-boy. It roved from door-step to door-step, in the arms of little Johnny Tetterby, and lagged heavily at the rear of troops of juveniles who followed the Tumblers or the Monkey, and came up, all on one side, a little too late for everything that was attractive, from Monday morning until Saturday night. Wherever childhood congregated to play, there was little Moloch making Johnny fag and toil. Wherever Johnny desired to stay, little Moloch became fractious, and would not remain. Whenever Johnny wanted to go out, Moloch was asleep, and must be watched. Whenever Johnny wanted to stay at home, Moloch was awake, and must be taken out. Yet Johnny was verily persuaded that it was a faultless baby, without its peer in the realm of England, and was quite content to catch meek glimpses of things in general from behind its skirts, or over its limp flapping bonnet, and to go staggering about with it like a very little porter with a very large parcel, which was not directed to anybody, and could never be delivered anywhere.

The small man who sat in the small parlour, making fruitless attempts to read his newspaper peaceably in the midst of this disturbance, was the father of the family, and the chief of the firm described in the inscription over the little shop front, by the name and title of A. TETTERBY AND CO., NEWSMEN. Indeed, strictly speaking, he was the only personage answering to that designation, as Co. was a mere poetical abstraction, altogether baseless and impersonal.

Tetterby's was the corner shop in Jerusalem Buildings. There was a good show of literature in the window, chiefly consisting of picture-newspapers out of date, and serial pirates, and footpads. Walking-sticks, likewise, and marbles, were included in the stock in trade. It had once extended into the light confectionery line; but it would seem that those elegancies of life were not in demand about Jerusalem Buildings, for nothing connected with that branch of commerce remained in the window, except a sort of small glass lantern containing a languishing mass of bull's-eyes, which had melted in the summer and congealed in the winter until all hope of ever getting them out, or of eating them without eating the lantern too, was gone for ever. Tetterby's had tried its hand at several things. It had once made a feeble little dart at the toy business; for, in another lantern, there was a heap of minute wax dolls, all sticking together upside down, in the direst confusion, with their feet on one another's heads, and a precipitate of broken arms and legs at the bottom. It had made a move in the millinery direction, which a few dry, wiry bonnet-shapes remained in a corner of the window to attest. It had fancied that a living might lie hidden in the tobacco trade, and had stuck up a representation of a native of each of the three integral portions of the British Empire, in the act of consuming that fragrant weed; with a poetic legend attached, importing that united in one cause they sat and joked, one chewed tobacco, one took snuff, one smoked: but nothing seemed to have come of it--except flies. Time had been when it had put a forlorn trust in imitative jewellery, for in one pane of glass there was a card of cheap seals, and another of pencil-cases, and a mysterious black amulet of inscrutable intention, labelled ninepence. But, to that hour, Jerusalem Buildings had bought none of them. In short, Tetterby's had tried so hard to get a livelihood out of Jerusalem Buildings in one way or other, and appeared to have done so indifferently in all, that the best position in the firm was too evidently Co.'s; Co., as a bodiless creation, being untroubled with the vulgar inconveniences of hunger and thirst, being chargeable neither to the poor's-rates nor the assessed taxes, and having no young family to provide for.

Tetterby himself, however, in his little parlour, as already mentioned, having the presence of a young family impressed upon his mind in a manner too clamorous to be disregarded, or to comport with the quiet perusal of a newspaper, laid down his paper, wheeled, in his distraction, a few times round the parlour, like an unde-cided carrier-pigeon, made an ineffectual rush at one or two flying little figures in bed-gowns that skimmed past him, and then, bearing suddenly down upon the only unoffending member of the family, boxed the ears of little Moloch's nurse.

"You bad boy!" said Mr. Tetterby, "haven't you any feeling for your poor father after the fatigues and anxieties of a hard winter's day, since five o'clock in the morn-ing, but must you wither his rest, and corrode his latest intelligence, with YOUR wicious tricks? Isn't it enough, sir, that your brother 'Dolphus is toiling and moiling in the fog and cold, and you rolling in the lap of luxury with a--with a baby, and everything you can wish for," said Mr. Tetterby, heaping this up as a great climax of blessings, "but must you make a wilderness of home, and maniacs of your parents? Must you, Johnny? Hey?" At each interrogation, Mr. Tetterby made a feint of boxing his ears again, but thought better of it, and held his hand.

"Oh, father!" whimpered Johnny, "when I wasn't doing anything, I'm sure, but taking such care of Sally, and getting her to sleep. Oh, father!"

"I wish my little woman would come home!" said Mr. Tetterby, relenting and repenting, "I only wish my little woman would come home! I ain't fit to deal with 'em. They make my head go round, and get the better of me. Oh, Johnny! Isn't it enough that your dear mother has provided you with that sweet sister?" indicating Moloch; "isn't it enough that you were seven boys before without a ray of gal, and that your dear mother went through what she DID go through, on purpose that you might all of you have a little sister, but must you so behave yourself as to make my head swim?"

Softening more and more, as his own tender feelings and those of his injured son were worked on, Mr. Tetterby concluded by embracing him, and immediately breaking away to catch one of the real delinquents. A reasonably good start occurring, he succeeded, after a short but smart run, and some rather severe cross-country work under and over the bedsteads, and in and out among the intricacies of the chairs, in capturing this infant, whom he condignly punished, and bore to bed. This example had a powerful, and apparently, mesmeric influence on him of the boots, who instantly fell into a deep sleep, though he had been, but a moment before, broad awake, and in the highest possible feather. Nor was it lost upon the two young architects, who retired to bed, in an adjoining closet, with great privacy and speed. The comrade of the Intercepted One also shrinking into his nest with similar discretion, Mr. Tetterby, when he paused for breath, found himself unexpectedly in a scene of peace.

"My little woman herself," said Mr. Tetterby, wiping his flushed face, "could hardly have done it better! I only wish my little woman had had it to do, I do indeed!"

Mr. Tetterby sought upon his screen for a passage appropriate to be impressed upon his children's minds on the occasion, and read the following.

"'It is an undoubted fact that all remarkable men have had remarkable mothers, and have respected them in after life as their best friends.' Think of your own remarkable mother, my boys," said Mr. Tetterby, "and know her value while she is still among you!"

He sat down again in his chair by the fire, and composed himself, cross-legged, over his newspaper.

"Let anybody, I don't care who it is, get out of bed again," said Tetterby, as a general proclamation, delivered in a very soft- hearted manner, "and astonishment will be the portion of that respected contemporary!"--which expression Mr. Tetterby selected from his screen. "Johnny, my child, take care of your only sister, Sally; for she's the brightest gem that ever sparkled on your early brow."

Johnny sat down on a little stool, and devotedly crushed himself beneath the weight of Moloch.

"Ah, what a gift that baby is to you, Johnny!" said his father, "and how thankful you ought to be! 'It is not generally known, Johnny,'" he was now referring to the screen again, "'but it is a fact ascertained, by accurate calculations, that the following immense percentage of babies never attain to two years old; that is to say--'"

"Oh, don't, father, please!" cried Johnny. "I can't bear it, when I think of Sally."

Mr. Tetterby desisting, Johnny, with a profound sense of his trust, wiped his eyes, and hushed his sister.

"Your brother 'Dolphus," said his father, poking the fire, "is late to-night, Johnny, and will come home like a lump of ice. What's got your precious mother?"

"Here's mother, and 'Dolphus too, father!" exclaimed Johnny, "I think."

"You're right!" returned his father, listening. "Yes, that's the footstep of my little woman."

The process of induction, by which Mr Tetterby had come to the conclusion that his wife was a little woman, was his own secret. She would have made two editions of himself, very easily. Considered as an individual, she was rather remarkable for being robust and portly; but considered with reference to her husband, her dimensions became magnificent. Nor did they assume a less imposing proportion, when studied with reference to the size of her seven sons, who were but diminutive. In the case of Sally, however, Mrs. Tetterby had asserted herself, at last; as nobody knew better than the victim Johnny, who weighed and measured that exacting idol every hour in the day.

Mrs. Tetterby, who had been marketing, and carried a basket, threw back her bonnet and shawl, and sitting down, fatigued, commanded Johnny to bring his sweet charge to her straightway, for a kiss. Johnny having complied, and gone back to his stool, and again crushed himself, Master Adolphus Tetterby, who had by this time unwound his torso out of a prismatic comforter, apparently interminable, requested the same favour. Johnny having again complied, and again gone back to his stool, and again crushed himself, Mr. Tetterby, struck by a sudden thought, preferred the same claim on his own parental part. The satisfaction of this third desire completely exhausted the sacrifice, who had hardly breath enough left to get back to his stool, crush himself again, and pant at his relations.

"Whatever you do, Johnny," said Mrs. Tetterby, shaking her head, "take care of her, or never look your mother in the face again."

"Nor your brother," said Adolphus.

"Nor your father, Johnny," added Mr. Tetterby.

Johnny, much affected by this conditional renunciation of him, looked down at Moloch's eyes to see that they were all right, so far, and skilfully patted her back (which was uppermost), and rocked her with his foot.

"Are you wet, 'Dolphus, my boy?" said his father. "Come and take my chair, and dry yourself."

"No, father, thank'ee," said Adolphus, smoothing himself down with his hands. "I an't very wet, I don't think. Does my face shine much, father?"

"Well, it DOES look waxy, my boy," returned Mr. Tetterby.

"It's the weather, father," said Adolphus, polishing his cheeks on the worn sleeve of his jacket. "What with rain, and sleet, and wind, and snow, and fog, my face gets quite brought out into a rash sometimes. And shines, it does--oh, don't it, though!"

Master Adolphus was also in the newspaper line of life, being employed, by a more thriving firm than his father and Co., to vend newspapers at a railway station, where his chubby little person, like a shabbily-disguised Cupid, and his shrill little voice (he was not much more than ten years old), were as well known as the hoarse panting of the locomotives, running in and out. His juvenility might have been at some loss for a harmless outlet, in this early application to traffic, but for a fortunate discovery he made of a means of entertaining himself, and of dividing the long day into stages of interest, without neglecting business. This ingenious invention, remarkable, like many great discoveries, for its simplicity, consisted in varying the first vowel in the word "paper," and substituting, in its stead, at different periods of the day, all the other vowels in grammatical succession. Thus, before daylight in the winter-time, he went to and fro, in his little oilskin cap and cape, and his big comforter, piercing the heavy air with his cry of "Morn-ing Pa-per!" which, about an hour before noon, changed to "Morn-ing Pepper!" which, at about two, changed to "Morn-ing Pip-per!" which in a couple of hours changed to "Morn-ing Pop-per!" and so declined with the sun into "Eve-ning Pup-per!" to the great relief and comfort of this young gentleman's spirits.

Mrs. Tetterby, his lady-mother, who had been sitting with her bonnet and shawl thrown back, as aforesaid, thoughtfully turning her wedding-ring round and round upon her finger, now rose, and divesting herself of her out-of-door attire, began to lay the cloth for supper.

"Ah, dear me, dear me, dear me!" said Mrs. Tetterby. "That's the way the world goes!"

"Which is the way the world goes, my dear?" asked Mr. Tetterby, looking round.

"Oh, nothing," said Mrs. Tetterby.

Mr. Tetterby elevated his eyebrows, folded his newspaper afresh, and carried his eyes up it, and down it, and across it, but was wandering in his attention, and not reading it.

Mrs. Tetterby, at the same time, laid the cloth, but rather as if she were punishing the table than preparing the family supper; hitting it unnecessarily hard with the knives and forks, slapping it with the plates, dinting it with the salt-cellar, and coming heavily down upon it with the loaf.

"Ah, dear me, dear me, dear me!" said Mrs. Tetterby. "That's the way the world goes!"

"My duck," returned her husband, looking round again, "you said that before. Which is the way the world goes?"

"Oh, nothing!" said Mrs. Tetterby.

"Sophia!" remonstrated her husband, "you said THAT before, too."

"Well, I'll say it again if you like," returned Mrs. Tetterby. "Oh nothing--there! And again if you like, oh nothing--there! And again if you like, oh nothing--now then!"

Mr. Tetterby brought his eye to bear upon the partner of his bosom, and said, in mild astonishment:

"My little woman, what has put you out?"

"I'm sure *I* don't know," she retorted. "Don't ask me. Who said I was put out at all? *I* never did."

Mr. Tetterby gave up the perusal of his newspaper as a bad job, and, taking a slow walk across the room, with his hands behind him, and his shoulders raised-- his gait according perfectly with the resignation of his manner--addressed himself to his two eldest offspring.

"Your supper will be ready in a minute, 'Dolphus," said Mr. Tetterby. "Your mother has been out in the wet, to the cook's shop, to buy it. It was very good of your mother so to do. YOU shall get some supper too, very soon, Johnny. Your mother's pleased with you, my man, for being so attentive to your precious sister."

Mrs. Tetterby, without any remark, but with a decided subsidence of her animosity towards the table, finished her preparations, and took, from her ample basket, a substantial slab of hot pease pudding wrapped in paper, and a basin covered with a saucer, which, on being uncovered, sent forth an odour so agreeable, that the three pair of eyes in the two beds opened wide and fixed themselves upon the banquet. Mr. Tetterby, without regarding this tacit invitation to be seated, stood repeating slowly, "Yes, yes, your supper will be ready in a minute, 'Dolphus--your mother went out in the wet, to the cook's shop, to buy it. It was very good of your mother so to do"--until Mrs. Tetterby, who had been exhibiting sundry tokens of contrition behind him, caught him round the neck, and wept.

"Oh, Dolphus!" said Mrs. Tetterby, "how could I go and behave so?"

This reconciliation affected Adolphus the younger and Johnny to that degree, that they both, as with one accord, raised a dismal cry, which had the effect of immediately shutting up the round eyes in the beds, and utterly routing the two remaining little Tetterbys, just then stealing in from the adjoining closet to see what was going on in the eating way.

"I am sure, 'Dolphus," sobbed Mrs. Tetterby, "coming home, I had no more idea than a child unborn--"

Mr. Tetterby seemed to dislike this figure of speech, and observed, "Say than the baby, my dear."

"--Had no more idea than the baby," said Mrs. Tetterby.--"Johnny, don't look at me, but look at her, or she'll fall out of your lap and be killed, and then you'll die in agonies of a broken heart, and serve you right.--No more idea I hadn't than that darling, of being cross when I came home; but somehow, 'Dolphus--" Mrs. Tetterby paused, and again turned her wedding-ring round and round upon her finger.

"I see!" said Mr. Tetterby. "I understand! My little woman was put out. Hard times, and hard weather, and hard work, make it trying now and then. I see, bless your soul! No wonder! Dolf, my man," continued Mr. Tetterby, exploring the basin with a fork, "here's your mother been and bought, at the cook's shop, besides pease pudding, a whole knuckle of a lovely roast leg of pork, with lots of crackling left upon it, and with seasoning gravy and mustard quite unlimited. Hand in your plate, my boy, and begin while it's simmering."

Master Adolphus, needing no second summons, received his portion with eyes rendered moist by appetite, and withdrawing to his particular stool, fell upon his supper tooth and nail. Johnny was not forgotten, but received his rations on bread, lest he should, in a flush of gravy, trickle any on the baby. He was required, for similar reasons, to keep his pudding, when not on active service, in his pocket.

There might have been more pork on the knucklebone,--which knucklebone the carver at the cook's shop had assuredly not forgotten in carving for previous customers--but there was no stint of seasoning, and that is an accessory dreamily suggesting pork, and pleasantly cheating the sense of taste. The pease pudding, too, the gravy and mustard, like the Eastern rose in respect of the nightingale, if they were not absolutely pork, had lived near it; so, upon the whole, there was the fla-vour of a middle-sized pig. It was irresistible to the Tetterbys in bed, who, though professing to slumber peacefully, crawled out when unseen by their parents, and silently appealed to their brothers for any gastronomic token of fraternal affection. They, not hard of heart, presenting scraps in return, it resulted that a party of light skirmishers in nightgowns were careering about the parlour all through supper, which harassed Mr. Tetterby exceedingly, and once or twice imposed upon him the necessity of a charge, before which these guerilla troops retired in all directions and in great confusion.

Mrs. Tetterby did not enjoy her supper. There seemed to be something on Mrs. Tetterby's mind. At one time she laughed without reason, and at another time she cried without reason, and at last she laughed and cried together in a manner so very unreasonable that her husband was confounded.

"My little woman," said Mr. Tetterby, "if the world goes that way, it appears to go the wrong way, and to choke you."

"Give me a drop of water," said Mrs. Tetterby, struggling with herself, "and don't speak to me for the present, or take any notice of me. Don't do it!"

Mr. Tetterby having administered the water, turned suddenly on the unlucky Johnny (who was full of sympathy), and demanded why he was wallowing there, in gluttony and idleness, instead of coming forward with the baby, that the sight of her might revive his mother. Johnny immediately approached, borne down by its weight; but Mrs. Tetterby holding out her hand to signify that she was not in a condition to bear that trying appeal to her feelings, he was interdicted from advancing another inch, on pain of perpetual hatred from all his dearest connections; and accordingly retired to his stool again, and crushed himself as before.

After a pause, Mrs. Tetterby said she was better now, and began to laugh.

"My little woman," said her husband, dubiously, "are you quite sure you're better? Or are you, Sophia, about to break out in a fresh direction?"

"No, 'Dolphus, no," replied his wife. "I'm quite myself." With that, settling her hair, and pressing the palms of her hands upon her eyes, she laughed again.

"What a wicked fool I was, to think so for a moment!" said Mrs. Tetterby. "Come nearer, 'Dolphus, and let me ease my mind, and tell you what I mean. Let me tell you all about it."

Mr. Tetterby bringing his chair closer, Mrs. Tetterby laughed again, gave him a hug, and wiped her eyes.

"You know, Dolphus, my dear," said Mrs. Tetterby, "that when I was single, I might have given myself away in several directions. At one time, four after me at once; two of them were sons of Mars."

"We're all sons of Ma's, my dear," said Mr. Tetterby, "jointly with Pa's."

"I don't mean that," replied his wife, "I mean soldiers-- serjeants."

"Oh!" said Mr. Tetterby.

"Well, 'Dolphus, I'm sure I never think of such things now, to regret them; and I'm sure I've got as good a husband, and would do as much to prove that I was fond of him, as--"

"As any little woman in the world," said Mr. Tetterby. "Very good. VERY good."

If Mr. Tetterby had been ten feet high, he could not have expressed a gentler consideration for Mrs. Tetterby's fairy-like stature; and if Mrs. Tetterby had been two feet high, she could not have felt it more appropriately her due.

"But you see, 'Dolphus," said Mrs. Tetterby, "this being Christmas- time, when all people who can, make holiday, and when all people who have got money, like to spend some, I did, somehow, get a little out of sorts when I was in the streets just now. There were so many things to be sold--such delicious things to eat, such fine things to look at, such delightful things to have--and there was so much calculat- ing and calculating necessary, before I durst lay out a sixpence for the commonest thing; and the basket was so large, and wanted so much in it; and my stock of money was so small, and would go such a little way;--you hate me, don't you, 'Dolphus?"

"Not quite," said Mr. Tetterby, "as yet."

"Well! I'll tell you the whole truth," pursued his wife, penitently, "and then perhaps you will. I felt all this, so much, when I was trudging about in the cold, and when I saw a lot of other calculating faces and large baskets trudging about, too, that I began to think whether I mightn't have done better, and been happier, if--I--hadn't--" the wedding-ring went round again, and Mrs. Tetterby shook her downcast head as she turned it.

"I see," said her husband quietly; "if you hadn't married at all, or if you had married somebody else?"

"Yes," sobbed Mrs. Tetterby. "That's really what I thought. Do you hate me now, 'Dolphus?"

"Why no," said Mr. Tetterby. "I don't find that I do, as yet."

Mrs. Tetterby gave him a thankful kiss, and went on.

"I begin to hope you won't, now, 'Dolphus, though I'm afraid I haven't told you the worst. I can't think what came over me. I don't know whether I was ill, or mad, or what I was, but I couldn't call up anything that seemed to bind us to each other, or to reconcile me to my fortune. All the pleasures and enjoyments we had ever had--THEY seemed so poor and insignificant, I hated them. I could have trodden on them. And I could think of nothing else, except our being poor, and the number of mouths there were at home."

"Well, well, my dear," said Mr. Tetterby, shaking her hand encouragingly, "that's truth, after all. We ARE poor, and there ARE a number of mouths at home here."

"Ah! but, Dolf, Dolf!" cried his wife, laying her hands upon his neck, "my good, kind, patient fellow, when I had been at home a very little while--how different! Oh, Dolf, dear, how different it was! I felt as if there was a rush of recollection on me, all at once, that softened my hard heart, and filled it up till it was bursting. All our struggles for a livelihood, all our cares and wants since we have been married, all the times of sickness, all the hours of watching, we have ever had, by one another, or by the children, seemed to speak to me, and say that they had made us one, and that I never might have been, or could have been, or would have been, any other than the wife and mother I am. Then, the cheap enjoyments that I could have trodden on so cruelly, got to be so precious to me--Oh so priceless, and dear!--that I couldn't bear to think how much I had wronged them; and I said, and say again a hundred times, how could I ever behave so, 'Dolphus, how could I ever have the heart to do it!"

The good woman, quite carried away by her honest tenderness and remorse, was weeping with all her heart, when she started up with a scream, and ran behind her husband. Her cry was so terrified, that the children started from their sleep and from their beds, and clung about her. Nor did her gaze belie her voice, as she pointed to a pale man in a black cloak who had come into the room.

"Look at that man! Look there! What does he want?"

"My dear," returned her husband, "I'll ask him if you'll let me go. What's the matter! How you shake!"

"I saw him in the street, when I was out just now. He looked at me, and stood near me. I am afraid of him."

"Afraid of him! Why?"

"I don't know why--I--stop! husband!" for he was going towards the stranger.

She had one hand pressed upon her forehead, and one upon her breast; and there was a peculiar fluttering all over her, and a hurried unsteady motion of her eyes, as if she had lost something.

"Are you ill, my dear?"

"What is it that is going from me again?" she muttered, in a low voice. "What IS this that is going away?"

Then she abruptly answered: "Ill? No, I am quite well," and stood looking vacantly at the floor.

Her husband, who had not been altogether free from the infection of her fear at first, and whom the present strangeness of her manner did not tend to reassure, addressed himself to the pale visitor in the black cloak, who stood still, and whose eyes were bent upon the ground.

"What may be your pleasure, sir," he asked, "with us?"

"I fear that my coming in unperceived," returned the visitor, "has alarmed you; but you were talking and did not hear me."

"My little woman says--perhaps you heard her say it," returned Mr. Tetterby, "that it's not the first time you have alarmed her to- night."

"I am sorry for it. I remember to have observed her, for a few moments only, in the street. I had no intention of frightening her."

As he raised his eyes in speaking, she raised hers. It was extraordinary to see what dread she had of him, and with what dread he observed it--and yet how narrowly and closely.

"My name," he said, "is Redlaw. I come from the old college hard by. A young gentleman who is a student there, lodges in your house, does he not?"

"Mr. Denham?" said Tetterby.

"Yes."

It was a natural action, and so slight as to be hardly noticeable; but the little man, before speaking again, passed his hand across his forehead, and looked quickly round the room, as though he were sensible of some change in its atmosphere. The Chemist, instantly transferring to him the look of dread he had directed towards the wife, stepped back, and his face turned paler.

"The gentleman's room," said Tetterby, "is upstairs, sir. There's a more convenient private entrance; but as you have come in here, it will save your going out into the cold, if you'll take this little staircase," showing one communicating directly with the parlour, "and go up to him that way, if you wish to see him."

"Yes, I wish to see him," said the Chemist. "Can you spare a light?"

The watchfulness of his haggard look, and the inexplicable distrust that darkened it, seemed to trouble Mr. Tetterby. He paused; and looking fixedly at him in return, stood for a minute or so, like a man stupefied, or fascinated.

At length he said, "I'll light you, sir, if you'll follow me."

"No," replied the Chemist, "I don't wish to be attended, or announced to him. He does not expect me. I would rather go alone. Please to give me the light, if you can spare it, and I'll find the way."

In the quickness of his expression of this desire, and in taking the candle from the newsman, he touched him on the breast. Withdrawing his hand hastily, almost as though he had wounded him by accident (for he did not know in what part of himself his new power resided, or how it was communicated, or how the manner of its reception varied in different persons), he turned and ascended the stair.

But when he reached the top, he stopped and looked down. The wife was standing in the same place, twisting her ring round and round upon her finger. The husband, with his head bent forward on his breast, was musing heavily and sullenly. The children, still clustering about the mother, gazed timidly after the visitor, and nestled together when they saw him looking down.

"Come!" said the father, roughly. "There's enough of this. Get to bed here!"

"The place is inconvenient and small enough," the mother added, "without you. Get to bed!"

The whole brood, scared and sad, crept away; little Johnny and the baby lagging last. The mother, glancing contemptuously round the sordid room, and tossing from her the fragments of their meal, stopped on the threshold of her task of clearing the table, and sat down, pondering idly and dejectedly. The father betook himself to the chimney-corner, and impatiently raking the small fire together, bent over it as if he would monopolise it all. They did not interchange a word.

The Chemist, paler than before, stole upward like a thief; looking back upon the change below, and dreading equally to go on or return.

"What have I done!" he said, confusedly. "What am I going to do!"

"To be the benefactor of mankind," he thought he heard a voice reply.

He looked round, but there was nothing there; and a passage now shutting out the little parlour from his view, he went on, directing his eyes before him at the way he went.

"It is only since last night," he muttered gloomily, "that I have remained shut up, and yet all things are strange to me. I am strange to myself. I am here, as in a dream. What interest have I in this place, or in any place that I can bring to my remembrance? My mind is going blind!"

There was a door before him, and he knocked at it. Being invited, by a voice within, to enter, he complied.

"Is that my kind nurse?" said the voice. "But I need not ask her. There is no one else to come here."

It spoke cheerfully, though in a languid tone, and attracted his attention to a young man lying on a couch, drawn before the chimney-piece, with the back towards the door. A meagre scanty stove, pinched and hollowed like a sick man's cheeks, and bricked into the centre of a hearth that it could scarcely warm, contained the fire, to which his face was turned. Being so near the windy house-top, it wasted quickly, and with a busy sound, and the burning ashes dropped down fast.

"They chink when they shoot out here," said the student, smiling, "so, according to the gossips, they are not coffins, but purses. I shall be well and rich yet, some day, if it please God, and shall live perhaps to love a daughter Milly, in remembrance of the kindest nature and the gentlest heart in the world."

He put up his hand as if expecting her to take it, but, being weakened, he lay still, with his face resting on his other hand, and did not turn round.

The Chemist glanced about the room;--at the student's books and papers, piled upon a table in a corner, where they, and his extinguished reading-lamp, now prohibited and put away, told of the attentive hours that had gone before this illness, and perhaps caused it;--at such signs of his old health and freedom, as the out-of-door attire that hung idle on the wall;--at those remembrances of other and less solitary scenes, the little miniatures upon the chimney-piece, and the drawing of home;--at that token of his emulation, perhaps, in some sort, of his personal attachment too, the framed engraving of himself, the looker-on. The time had been, only yesterday, when not one of these objects, in its remotest association of interest with the living figure before him, would have been lost on Redlaw. Now, they were but objects; or, if any gleam of such connexion shot upon him, it perplexed, and not enlightened him, as he stood looking round with a dull wonder.

The student, recalling the thin hand which had remained so long untouched, raised himself on the couch, and turned his head.

"Mr. Redlaw!" he exclaimed, and started up.

Redlaw put out his arm.

"Don't come nearer to me. I will sit here. Remain you, where you are!"

He sat down on a chair near the door, and having glanced at the young man standing leaning with his hand upon the couch, spoke with his eyes averted towards the ground.

"I heard, by an accident, by what accident is no matter, that one of my class was ill and solitary. I received no other description of him, than that he lived in this street. Beginning my inquiries at the first house in it, I have found him."

"I have been ill, sir," returned the student, not merely with a modest hesitation, but with a kind of awe of him, "but am greatly better. An attack of fever--of the brain, I believe--has weakened me, but I am much better. I cannot say I have been solitary, in my illness, or I should forget the ministering hand that has been near me."

"You are speaking of the keeper's wife," said Redlaw.

"Yes." The student bent his head, as if he rendered her some silent homage.

The Chemist, in whom there was a cold, monotonous apathy, which rendered him more like a marble image on the tomb of the man who had started from his dinner yesterday at the first mention of this student's case, than the breathing man himself, glanced again at the student leaning with his hand upon the couch, and looked upon the ground, and in the air, as if for light for his blinded mind.

"I remembered your name," he said, "when it was mentioned to me down stairs, just now; and I recollect your face. We have held but very little personal communication together?"

"Very little."

"You have retired and withdrawn from me, more than any of the rest, I think?"

The student signified assent.

"And why?" said the Chemist; not with the least expression of interest, but with a moody, wayward kind of curiosity. "Why? How comes it that you have sought to keep especially from me, the knowledge of your remaining here, at this season, when all the rest have dispersed, and of your being ill? I want to know why this is?"

The young man, who had heard him with increasing agitation, raised his down-cast eyes to his face, and clasping his hands together, cried with sudden earnestness and with trembling lips:

"Mr. Redlaw! You have discovered me. You know my secret!"

"Secret?" said the Chemist, harshly. "I know?"

"Yes! Your manner, so different from the interest and sympathy which endear you to so many hearts, your altered voice, the constraint there is in everything you say, and in your looks," replied the student, "warn me that you know me. That you would conceal it, even now, is but a proof to me (God knows I need none!) of your natural kindness and of the bar there is between us."

A vacant and contemptuous laugh, was all his answer.

"But, Mr. Redlaw," said the student, "as a just man, and a good man, think how innocent I am, except in name and descent, of participation in any wrong inflicted on you or in any sorrow you have borne."

"Sorrow!" said Redlaw, laughing. "Wrong! What are those to me?"

"For Heaven's sake," entreated the shrinking student, "do not let the mere in-terchange of a few words with me change you like this, sir! Let me pass again from your knowledge and notice. Let me occupy my old reserved and distant place among those whom you instruct. Know me only by the name I have assumed, and not by that of Longford--"

"Longford!" exclaimed the other.

He clasped his head with both his hands, and for a moment turned upon the young man his own intelligent and thoughtful face. But the light passed from it, like the sun-beam of an instant, and it clouded as before.

"The name my mother bears, sir," faltered the young man, "the name she took, when she might, perhaps, have taken one more honoured. Mr. Redlaw," hesitating, "I believe I know that history. Where my information halts, my guesses at what is wanting may supply something not remote from the truth. I am the child of a marriage that has not proved itself a well-assorted or a happy one. From infancy, I have heard you spoken of with honour and respect--with something that was almost reverence. I have heard of such devotion, of such fortitude and tenderness, of such rising up against the obstacles which press men down, that my fancy, since I learnt my little lesson from my mother, has shed a lustre on your name. At last, a poor student myself, from whom could I learn but you?"

Redlaw, unmoved, unchanged, and looking at him with a staring frown, answered by no word or sign.

"I cannot say," pursued the other, "I should try in vain to say, how much it has impressed me, and affected me, to find the gracious traces of the past, in that certain power of winning gratitude and confidence which is associated among us students (among the humblest of us, most) with Mr. Redlaw's generous name. Our ages and positions are so different, sir, and I am so accustomed to regard you from a distance, that I wonder at my own presumption when I touch, however lightly, on that theme. But to one who--I may say, who felt no common interest in my mother once--it may be something to hear, now that all is past, with what indescribable feelings of affection I have, in my obscurity, regarded him; with what pain and reluctance I have kept aloof from his encouragement, when a word of it would have made me rich; yet how I have felt it fit that I should hold my course, content to know him, and to be unknown. Mr. Redlaw," said the student, faintly, "what I would have said, I have said ill, for my strength is strange to me as yet; but for anything unworthy in this fraud of mine, forgive me, and for all the rest forget me!"

The staring frown remained on Redlaw's face, and yielded to no other expression until the student, with these words, advanced towards him, as if to touch his hand, when he drew back and cried to him:

"Don't come nearer to me!"

The young man stopped, shocked by the eagerness of his recoil, and by the sternness of his repulsion; and he passed his hand, thoughtfully, across his forehead.

"The past is past," said the Chemist. "It dies like the brutes. Who talks to me of its traces in my life? He raves or lies! What have I to do with your distempered dreams? If you want money, here it is. I came to offer it; and that is all I came for. There can be nothing else that brings me here," he muttered, holding his head again, with both his hands. "There CAN be nothing else, and yet--"

He had tossed his purse upon the table. As he fell into this dim cogitation with himself, the student took it up, and held it out to him.

"Take it back, sir," he said proudly, though not angrily. "I wish you could take from me, with it, the remembrance of your words and offer."

"You do?" he retorted, with a wild light in his eyes. "You do?"

"I do!"

The Chemist went close to him, for the first time, and took the purse, and turned him by the arm, and looked him in the face.

"There is sorrow and trouble in sickness, is there not?" he demanded, with a laugh.

The wondering student answered, "Yes."

"In its unrest, in its anxiety, in its suspense, in all its train of physical and mental miseries?" said the Chemist, with a wild unearthly exultation. "All best forgotten, are they not?"

The student did not answer, but again passed his hand, confusedly, across his forehead. Redlaw still held him by the sleeve, when Milly's voice was heard outside.

"I can see very well now," she said, "thank you, Dolf. Don't cry, dear. Father and mother will be comfortable again, to-morrow, and home will be comfortable too. A gentleman with him, is there!"

Redlaw released his hold, as he listened.

"I have feared, from the first moment," he murmured to himself, "to meet her. There is a steady quality of goodness in her, that I dread to influence. I may be the murderer of what is tenderest and best within her bosom."

She was knocking at the door.

"Shall I dismiss it as an idle foreboding, or still avoid her?" he muttered, looking uneasily around.

She was knocking at the door again.

"Of all the visitors who could come here," he said, in a hoarse alarmed voice, turning to his companion, "this is the one I should desire most to avoid. Hide me!"

The student opened a frail door in the wall, communicating where the garret-roof began to slope towards the floor, with a small inner room. Redlaw passed in hastily, and shut it after him.

The student then resumed his place upon the couch, and called to her to enter.

"Dear Mr. Edmund," said Milly, looking round, "they told me there was a gentleman here."

"There is no one here but I."

"There has been some one?"

"Yes, yes, there has been some one."

She put her little basket on the table, and went up to the back of the couch, as if to take the extended hand--but it was not there. A little surprised, in her quiet way, she leaned over to look at his face, and gently touched him on the brow.

"Are you quite as well to-night? Your head is not so cool as in the afternoon."

"Tut!" said the student, petulantly, "very little ails me."

A little more surprise, but no reproach, was expressed in her face, as she withdrew to the other side of the table, and took a small packet of needlework from her basket. But she laid it down again, on second thoughts, and going noiselessly about the room, set everything exactly in its place, and in the neatest order; even to the cushions on the couch, which she touched with so light a hand, that he hardly seemed to know it, as he lay looking at the fire. When all this was done, and she had swept the hearth, she sat down, in her modest little bonnet, to her work, and was quietly busy on it directly.

"It's the new muslin curtain for the window, Mr. Edmund," said Milly, stitching away as she talked. "It will look very clean and nice, though it costs very little, and will save your eyes, too, from the light. My William says the room should not be too light just now, when you are recovering so well, or the glare might make you giddy."

He said nothing; but there was something so fretful and impatient in his change of position, that her quick fingers stopped, and she looked at him anxiously.

"The pillows are not comfortable," she said, laying down her work and rising. "I will soon put them right."

"They are very well," he answered. "Leave them alone, pray. You make so much of everything."

He raised his head to say this, and looked at her so thanklessly, that, after he had thrown himself down again, she stood timidly pausing. However, she resumed her seat, and her needle, without having directed even a murmuring look towards him, and was soon as busy as before.

"I have been thinking, Mr. Edmund, that YOU have been often thinking of late, when I have been sitting by, how true the saying is, that adversity is a good teacher. Health will be more precious to you, after this illness, than it has ever been. And years hence, when this time of year comes round, and you remember the days when you lay here sick, alone, that the knowledge of your illness might not afflict those who are dearest to you, your home will be doubly dear and doubly blest. Now, isn't that a good, true thing?"

She was too intent upon her work, and too earnest in what she said, and too composed and quiet altogether, to be on the watch for any look he might direct towards her in reply; so the shaft of his ungrateful glance fell harmless, and did not wound her.

"Ah!" said Milly, with her pretty head inclining thoughtfully on one side, as she looked down, following her busy fingers with her eyes. "Even on me--and I am very different from you, Mr. Edmund, for I have no learning, and don't know how to think properly--this view of such things has made a great impression, since you have been lying ill. When I have seen you so touched by the kindness and attention of the poor people down stairs, I have felt that you thought even that experience some repayment for the loss of health, and I have read in your face, as plain as if it was a book, that but for some trouble and sorrow we should never know half the good there is about us."

His getting up from the couch, interrupted her, or she was going on to say more.

"We needn't magnify the merit, Mrs. William," he rejoined slightingly. "The people down stairs will be paid in good time I dare say, for any little extra service they may have rendered me; and perhaps they anticipate no less. I am much obliged to you, too."

Her fingers stopped, and she looked at him.

"I can't be made to feel the more obliged by your exaggerating the case," he said. "I am sensible that you have been interested in me, and I say I am much obliged to you. What more would you have?"

Her work fell on her lap, as she still looked at him walking to and fro with an intolerant air, and stopping now and then.

"I say again, I am much obliged to you. Why weaken my sense of what is your due in obligation, by preferring enormous claims upon me? Trouble, sorrow, affliction, adversity! One might suppose I had been dying a score of deaths here!"

"Do you believe, Mr. Edmund," she asked, rising and going nearer to him, "that I spoke of the poor people of the house, with any reference to myself? To me?" laying her hand upon her bosom with a simple and innocent smile of astonishment.

"Oh! I think nothing about it, my good creature," he returned. "I have had an indisposition, which your solicitude--observe! I say solicitude--makes a great deal more of, than it merits; and it's over, and we can't perpetuate it."

He coldly took a book, and sat down at the table.

She watched him for a little while, until her smile was quite gone, and then, returning to where her basket was, said gently:

"Mr. Edmund, would you rather be alone?"

"There is no reason why I should detain you here," he replied.

"Except--" said Milly, hesitating, and showing her work.

"Oh! the curtain," he answered, with a supercilious laugh. "That's not worth staying for."

She made up the little packet again, and put it in her basket. Then, standing before him with such an air of patient entreaty that he could not choose but look at her, she said:

"If you should want me, I will come back willingly. When you did want me, I was quite happy to come; there was no merit in it. I think you must be afraid, that, now you are getting well, I may be troublesome to you; but I should not have been, indeed. I should have come no longer than your weakness and confinement lasted. You owe me nothing; but it is right that you should deal as justly by me as if I was a lady--even the very lady that you love; and if you suspect me of meanly making much of the little I have tried to do to comfort your sick room, you do yourself more wrong than ever you can do me. That is why I am sorry. That is why I am very sorry."

If she had been as passionate as she was quiet, as indignant as she was calm, as angry in her look as she was gentle, as loud of tone as she was low and clear, she might have left no sense of her departure in the room, compared with that which fell upon the lonely student when she went away.

He was gazing drearily upon the place where she had been, when Redlaw came out of his concealment, and came to the door.

"When sickness lays its hand on you again," he said, looking fiercely back at him, "--may it be soon!--Die here! Rot here!"

"What have you done?" returned the other, catching at his cloak. "What change have you wrought in me? What curse have you brought upon me? Give me back MYself!"

"Give me back myself!" exclaimed Redlaw like a madman. "I am infected! I am infectious! I am charged with poison for my own mind, and the minds of all mankind. Where I felt interest, compassion, sympathy, I am turning into stone. Selfishness and ingratitude spring up in my blighting footsteps. I am only so much less base than the wretches whom I make so, that in the moment of their transformation I can hate them."

As he spoke--the young man still holding to his cloak--he cast him off, and struck him: then, wildly hurried out into the night air where the wind was blowing, the snow falling, the cloud-drift sweeping on, the moon dimly shining; and where, blowing in the wind, falling with the snow, drifting with the clouds, shining in the moonlight, and heavily looming in the darkness, were the Phantom's words, "The gift that I have given, you shall give again, go where you will!"

Whither he went, he neither knew nor cared, so that he avoided company. The change he felt within him made the busy streets a desert, and himself a desert, and the multitude around him, in their manifold endurances and ways of life, a mighty waste of sand, which the winds tossed into unintelligible heaps and made a ruinous confusion of. Those traces in his breast which the Phantom had told him would "die out soon," were not, as yet, so far upon their way to death, but that he understood enough of what he was, and what he made of others, to desire to be alone.

This put it in his mind--he suddenly bethought himself, as he was going along, of the boy who had rushed into his room. And then he recollected, that of those with whom he had communicated since the Phantom's disappearance, that boy alone had shown no sign of being changed.

Monstrous and odious as the wild thing was to him, he determined to seek it out, and prove if this were really so; and also to seek it with another intention, which came into his thoughts at the same time.

So, resolving with some difficulty where he was, he directed his steps back to the old college, and to that part of it where the general porch was, and where, alone, the pavement was worn by the tread of the students' feet.

The keeper's house stood just within the iron gates, forming a part of the chief quadrangle. There was a little cloister outside, and from that sheltered place he knew he could look in at the window of their ordinary room, and see who was within. The iron gates were shut, but his hand was familiar with the fastening, and drawing it back by thrusting in his wrist between the bars, he passed through softly, shut it again, and crept up to the window, crumbling the thin crust of snow with his feet.

The fire, to which he had directed the boy last night, shining brightly through the glass, made an illuminated place upon the ground. Instinctively avoiding this, and going round it, he looked in at the window. At first, he thought that there was no one there, and that the blaze was reddening only the old beams in the ceiling and the dark walls; but peering in more narrowly, he saw the object of his search coiled asleep before it on the floor. He passed quickly to the door, opened it, and went in.

The creature lay in such a fiery heat, that, as the Chemist stooped to rouse him, it scorched his head. So soon as he was touched, the boy, not half awake, clutching his rags together with the instinct of flight upon him, half rolled and half ran into a distant corner of the room, where, heaped upon the ground, he struck his foot out to defend himself.

"Get up!" said the Chemist. "You have not forgotten me?"

"You let me alone!" returned the boy. "This is the woman's house-- not yours."

The Chemist's steady eye controlled him somewhat, or inspired him with enough submission to be raised upon his feet, and looked at.

"Who washed them, and put those bandages where they were bruised and cracked?" asked the Chemist, pointing to their altered state.

"The woman did."

"And is it she who has made you cleaner in the face, too?"

"Yes, the woman."

Redlaw asked these questions to attract his eyes towards himself, and with the same intent now held him by the chin, and threw his wild hair back, though he loathed to touch him. The boy watched his eyes keenly, as if he thought it needful to his own defence, not knowing what he might do next; and Redlaw could see well that no change came over him.

"Where are they?" he inquired.

"The woman's out."

"I know she is. Where is the old man with the white hair, and his son?"

"The woman's husband, d'ye mean?" inquired the boy.

"Ay. Where are those two?"

"Out. Something's the matter, somewhere. They were fetched out in a hurry, and told me to stop here."

"Come with me," said the Chemist, "and I'll give you money."

"Come where? and how much will you give?"

"I'll give you more shillings than you ever saw, and bring you back soon. Do you know your way to where you came from?"

"You let me go," returned the boy, suddenly twisting out of his grasp. "I'm not a going to take you there. Let me be, or I'll heave some fire at you!"

He was down before it, and ready, with his savage little hand, to pluck the burning coals out.

What the Chemist had felt, in observing the effect of his charmed influence stealing over those with whom he came in contact, was not nearly equal to the cold vague terror with which he saw this baby- monster put it at defiance. It chilled his blood to look on the immovable impenetrable thing, in the likeness of a child, with its sharp malignant face turned up to his, and its almost infant hand, ready at the bars.

"Listen, boy!" he said. "You shall take me where you please, so that you take me where the people are very miserable or very wicked. I want to do them good, and not to harm them. You shall have money, as I have told you, and I will bring you back. Get up! Come quickly!" He made a hasty step towards the door, afraid of her returning.

"Will you let me walk by myself, and never hold me, nor yet touch me?" said the boy, slowly withdrawing the hand with which he threatened, and beginning to get up.

"I will!"

"And let me go, before, behind, or anyways I like?"

"I will!"

"Give me some money first, then, and go."

The Chemist laid a few shillings, one by one, in his extended hand. To count them was beyond the boy's knowledge, but he said "one," every time, and avariciously looked at each as it was given, and at the donor. He had nowhere to put them, out of his hand, but in his mouth; and he put them there.

Redlaw then wrote with his pencil on a leaf of his pocket-book, that the boy was with him; and laying it on the table, signed to him to follow. Keeping his rags together, as usual, the boy complied, and went out with his bare head and naked feet into the winter night.

Preferring not to depart by the iron gate by which he had entered, where they were in danger of meeting her whom he so anxiously avoided, the Chemist led the way, through some of those passages among which the boy had lost himself, and by that portion of the building where he lived, to a small door of which he had the key. When they got into the street, he stopped to ask his guide--who instantly retreated from him--if he knew where they were.

The savage thing looked here and there, and at length, nodding his head, pointed in the direction he designed to take. Redlaw going on at once, he followed, something less suspiciously; shifting his money from his mouth into his hand, and back again into his mouth, and stealthily rubbing it bright upon his shreds of dress, as he went along.

Three times, in their progress, they were side by side. Three times they stopped, being side by side. Three times the Chemist glanced down at his face, and shuddered as it forced upon him one reflection.

The first occasion was when they were crossing an old churchyard, and Redlaw stopped among the graves, utterly at a loss how to connect them with any tender, softening, or consolatory thought.

The second was, when the breaking forth of the moon induced him to look up at the Heavens, where he saw her in her glory, surrounded by a host of stars he still knew by the names and histories which human science has appended to them; but where he saw nothing else he had been wont to see, felt nothing he had been wont to feel, in looking up there, on a bright night.

The third was when he stopped to listen to a plaintive strain of music, but could only hear a tune, made manifest to him by the dry mechanism of the instruments and his own ears, with no address to any mystery within him, without a whisper in it of the past, or of the future, powerless upon him as the sound of last year's running water, or the rushing of last year's wind.

At each of these three times, he saw with horror that, in spite of the vast intellectual distance between them, and their being unlike each other in all physical respects, the expression on the boy's face was the expression on his own.

They journeyed on for some time--now through such crowded places, that he often looked over his shoulder thinking he had lost his guide, but generally finding him within his shadow on his other side; now by ways so quiet, that he could have counted his short, quick, naked footsteps coming on behind--until they arrived at a ruinous collection of houses, and the boy touched him and stopped.

"In there!" he said, pointing out one house where there were shattered lights in the windows, and a dim lantern in the doorway, with "Lodgings for Travellers" painted on it.

Redlaw looked about him; from the houses to the waste piece of ground on which the houses stood, or rather did not altogether tumble down, unfenced, undrained, unlighted, and bordered by a sluggish ditch; from that, to the sloping line of arches, part of some neighbouring viaduct or bridge with which it was surrounded, and which lessened gradually towards them, until the last but one was a mere kennel for a dog, the last a plundered little heap of bricks; from that, to the child, close to him, cowering and trembling with the cold, and limping on one little foot, while he coiled the other round his leg to warm it, yet staring at all these things with that frightful likeness of expression so apparent in his face, that Redlaw started from him.

"In there!" said the boy, pointing out the house again. "I'll wait."

"Will they let me in?" asked Redlaw.

"Say you're a doctor," he answered with a nod. "There's plenty ill here."

Looking back on his way to the house-door, Redlaw saw him trail himself upon the dust and crawl within the shelter of the smallest arch, as if he were a rat. He had no pity for the thing, but he was afraid of it; and when it looked out of its den at him, he hurried to the house as a retreat.

"Sorrow, wrong, and trouble," said the Chemist, with a painful effort at some more distinct remembrance, "at least haunt this place darkly. He can do no harm, who brings forgetfulness of such things here!"

With these words, he pushed the yielding door, and went in.

There was a woman sitting on the stairs, either asleep or forlorn, whose head was bent down on her hands and knees. As it was not easy to pass without treading on her, and as she was perfectly regardless of his near approach, he stopped, and touched her on the shoulder. Looking up, she showed him quite a young face, but one whose bloom and promise were all swept away, as if the haggard winter should unnaturally kill the spring.

With little or no show of concern on his account, she moved nearer to the wall to leave him a wider passage.

"What are you?" said Redlaw, pausing, with his hand upon the broken stair-rail.

"What do you think I am?" she answered, showing him her face again.

He looked upon the ruined Temple of God, so lately made, so soon disfigured; and something, which was not compassion--for the springs in which a true compassion for such miseries has its rise, were dried up in his breast--but which was nearer to it, for the moment, than any feeling that had lately struggled into the darkening, but not yet wholly darkened, night of his mind--mingled a touch of softness with his next words.

"I am come here to give relief, if I can," he said. "Are you thinking of any wrong?"

She frowned at him, and then laughed; and then her laugh prolonged itself into a shivering sigh, as she dropped her head again, and hid her fingers in her hair.

"Are you thinking of a wrong?" he asked once more.

"I am thinking of my life," she said, with a monetary look at him.

He had a perception that she was one of many, and that he saw the type of thousands, when he saw her, drooping at his feet.

"What are your parents?" he demanded.

"I had a good home once. My father was a gardener, far away, in the country."

"Is he dead?"

"He's dead to me. All such things are dead to me. You a gentleman, and not know that!" She raised her eyes again, and laughed at him.

"Girl!" said Redlaw, sternly, "before this death, of all such things, was brought about, was there no wrong done to you? In spite of all that you can do, does no remembrance of wrong cleave to you? Are there not times upon times when it is misery to you?"

So little of what was womanly was left in her appearance, that now, when she burst into tears, he stood amazed. But he was more amazed, and much disquieted, to note that in her awakened recollection of this wrong, the first trace of her old humanity and frozen tenderness appeared to show itself.

He drew a little off, and in doing so, observed that her arms were black, her face cut, and her bosom bruised.

"What brutal hand has hurt you so?" he asked.

"My own. I did it myself!" she answered quickly.

"It is impossible."

"I'll swear I did! He didn't touch me. I did it to myself in a passion, and threw myself down here. He wasn't near me. He never laid a hand upon me!"

In the white determination of her face, confronting him with this untruth, he saw enough of the last perversion and distortion of good surviving in that miserable breast, to be stricken with remorse that he had ever come near her.

"Sorrow, wrong, and trouble!" he muttered, turning his fearful gaze away. "All that connects her with the state from which she has fallen, has those roots! In the name of God, let me go by!"

Afraid to look at her again, afraid to touch her, afraid to think of having sundered the last thread by which she held upon the mercy of Heaven, he gathered his cloak about him, and glided swiftly up the stairs.

Opposite to him, on the landing, was a door, which stood partly open, and which, as he ascended, a man with a candle in his hand, came forward from within to shut. But this man, on seeing him, drew back, with much emotion in his manner, and, as if by a sudden impulse, mentioned his name aloud.

In the surprise of such a recognition there, he stopped, endeavouring to recollect the wan and startled face. He had no time to consider it, for, to his yet greater amazement, old Philip came out of the room, and took him by the hand.

"Mr. Redlaw," said the old man, "this is like you, this is like you, sir! you have heard of it, and have come after us to render any help you can. Ah, too late, too late!"

Redlaw, with a bewildered look, submitted to be led into the room. A man lay there, on a truckle-bed, and William Swidger stood at the bedside.

"Too late!" murmured the old man, looking wistfully into the Chemist's face; and the tears stole down his cheeks.

"That's what I say, father," interposed his son in a low voice. "That's where it is, exactly. To keep as quiet as ever we can while he's a dozing, is the only thing to do. You're right, father!"

Redlaw paused at the bedside, and looked down on the figure that was stretched upon the mattress. It was that of a man, who should have been in the vigour of his life, but on whom it was not likely the sun would ever shine again. The vices of his forty or fifty years' career had so branded him, that, in comparison with their effects upon his face, the heavy hand of Time upon the old man's face who watched him had been merciful and beautifying.

"Who is this?" asked the Chemist, looking round.

"My son George, Mr. Redlaw," said the old man, wringing his hands. "My eldest son, George, who was more his mother's pride than all the rest!"

Redlaw's eyes wandered from the old man's grey head, as he laid it down upon the bed, to the person who had recognised him, and who had kept aloof, in the remotest corner of the room. He seemed to be about his own age; and although he knew no such hopeless decay and broken man as he appeared to be, there was something in the turn of his figure, as he stood with his back towards him, and now went out at the door, that made him pass his hand uneasily across his brow.

"William," he said in a gloomy whisper, "who is that man?"

"Why you see, sir," returned Mr. William, "that's what I say, myself. Why should a man ever go and gamble, and the like of that, and let himself down inch by inch till he can't let himself down any lower!"

"Has HE done so?" asked Redlaw, glancing after him with the same uneasy action as before.

"Just exactly that, sir," returned William Swidger, "as I'm told. He knows a little about medicine, sir, it seems; and having been wayfaring towards London with my unhappy brother that you see here," Mr. William passed his coat-sleeve across his eyes, "and being lodging up stairs for the night--what I say, you see, is that strange companions come together here sometimes--he looked in to attend upon him, and came for us at his request. What a mournful spectacle, sir! But that's where it is. It's enough to kill my father!"

Redlaw looked up, at these words, and, recalling where he was and with whom, and the spell he carried with him--which his surprise had obscured--retired a little, hurriedly, debating with himself whether to shun the house that moment, or re-main.

Yielding to a certain sullen doggedness, which it seemed to be a part of his condition to struggle with, he argued for remaining.

"Was it only yesterday," he said, "when I observed the memory of this old man to be a tissue of sorrow and trouble, and shall I be afraid, to-night, to shake it? Are such remembrances as I can drive away, so precious to this dying man that I need fear for HIM? No! I'll stay here."

But he stayed in fear and trembling none the less for these words; and, shrouded in his black cloak with his face turned from them, stood away from the bedside, listening to what they said, as if he felt himself a demon in the place.

"Father!" murmured the sick man, rallying a little from stupor.

"My boy! My son George!" said old Philip.

"You spoke, just now, of my being mother's favourite, long ago. It's a dreadful thing to think now, of long ago!"

"No, no, no;" returned the old man. "Think of it. Don't say it's dreadful. It's not dreadful to me, my son."

"It cuts you to the heart, father." For the old man's tears were falling on him.

"Yes, yes," said Philip, "so it does; but it does me good. It's a heavy sorrow to think of that time, but it does me good, George. Oh, think of it too, think of it too, and your heart will be softened more and more! Where's my son William? William, my boy, your mother loved him dearly to the last, and with her latest breath said, 'Tell him I forgave him, blessed him, and prayed for him.' Those were her words to me. I have never forgotten them, and I'm eighty-seven!"

"Father!" said the man upon the bed, "I am dying, I know. I am so far gone, that I can hardly speak, even of what my mind most runs on. Is there any hope for me beyond this bed?"

"There is hope," returned the old man, "for all who are softened and penitent. There is hope for all such. Oh!" he exclaimed, clasping his hands and looking up, "I was thankful, only yesterday, that I could remember this unhappy son when he was an innocent child. But what a comfort it is, now, to think that even God himself has that remembrance of him!"

Redlaw spread his hands upon his face, and shrank, like a murderer.

"Ah!" feebly moaned the man upon the bed. "The waste since then, the waste of life since then!"

"But he was a child once," said the old man. "He played with children. Before he lay down on his bed at night, and fell into his guiltless rest, he said his prayers at his poor mother's knee. I have seen him do it, many a time; and seen her lay his head upon her breast, and kiss him. Sorrowful as it was to her and me, to think of this, when he went so wrong, and when our hopes and plans for him were all broken, this gave him still a hold upon us, that nothing else could have given. Oh, Father, so much better than the fathers upon earth! Oh, Father, so much more afflicted by the errors of Thy children! take this wanderer back! Not as he is, but as he was then, let him cry to Thee, as he has so often seemed to cry to us!"

As the old man lifted up his trembling hands, the son, for whom he made the supplication, laid his sinking head against him for support and comfort, as if he were indeed the child of whom he spoke.

When did man ever tremble, as Redlaw trembled, in the silence that ensued! He knew it must come upon them, knew that it was coming fast.

"My time is very short, my breath is shorter," said the sick man, supporting himself on one arm, and with the other groping in the air, "and I remember there is something on my mind concerning the man who was here just now, Father and William--wait!--is there really anything in black, out there?"

"Yes, yes, it is real," said his aged father.

"Is it a man?"

"What I say myself, George," interposed his brother, bending kindly over him. "It's Mr. Redlaw."

"I thought I had dreamed of him. Ask him to come here."

The Chemist, whiter than the dying man, appeared before him. Obedient to the motion of his hand, he sat upon the bed.

"It has been so ripped up, to-night, sir," said the sick man, laying his hand upon his heart, with a look in which the mute, imploring agony of his condition was concentrated, "by the sight of my poor old father, and the thought of all the trouble I have been the cause of, and all the wrong and sorrow lying at my door, that-- "

Was it the extremity to which he had come, or was it the dawning of another change, that made him stop?

"--that what I CAN do right, with my mind running on so much, so fast, I'll try to do. There was another man here. Did you see him?"

Redlaw could not reply by any word; for when he saw that fatal sign he knew so well now, of the wandering hand upon the forehead, his voice died at his lips. But he made some indication of assent.

"He is penniless, hungry, and destitute. He is completely beaten down, and has no resource at all. Look after him! Lose no time! I know he has it in his mind to kill himself."

It was working. It was on his face. His face was changing, hardening, deepening in all its shades, and losing all its sorrow.

"Don't you remember? Don't you know him?" he pursued.

He shut his face out for a moment, with the hand that again wandered over his forehead, and then it lowered on Redlaw, reckless, ruffianly, and callous.

"Why, d-n you!" he said, scowling round, "what have you been doing to me here! I have lived bold, and I mean to die bold. To the Devil with you!"

And so lay down upon his bed, and put his arms up, over his head and ears, as resolute from that time to keep out all access, and to die in his indifference.

If Redlaw had been struck by lightning, it could not have struck him from the bedside with a more tremendous shock. But the old man, who had left the bed while his son was speaking to him, now returning, avoided it quickly likewise, and with abhorrence.

"Where's my boy William?" said the old man hurriedly. "William, come away from here. We'll go home."

"Home, father!" returned William. "Are you going to leave your own son?"

"Where's my own son?" replied the old man.

"Where? why, there!"

"That's no son of mine," said Philip, trembling with resentment. "No such wretch as that, has any claim on me. My children are pleasant to look at, and they wait upon me, and get my meat and drink ready, and are useful to me. I've a right to it! I'm eighty-seven!"

"You're old enough to be no older," muttered William, looking at him grudgingly, with his hands in his pockets. "I don't know what good you are, myself. We could have a deal more pleasure without you."

"MY son, Mr. Redlaw!" said the old man. "MY son, too! The boy talking to me of MY son! Why, what has he ever done to give me any pleasure, I should like to know?"

"I don't know what you have ever done to give ME any pleasure," said William, sulkily.

"Let me think," said the old man. "For how many Christmas times running, have I sat in my warm place, and never had to come out in the cold night air; and have made good cheer, without being disturbed by any such uncomfortable, wretched sight as him there? Is it twenty, William?"

"Nigher forty, it seems," he muttered. "Why, when I look at my father, sir, and come to think of it," addressing Redlaw, with an impatience and irritation that were quite new, "I'm whipped if I can see anything in him but a calendar of ever so many years of eating and drinking, and making himself comfortable, over and over again."

"I--I'm eighty-seven," said the old man, rambling on, childishly and weakly, "and I don't know as I ever was much put out by anything. I'm not going to begin now, because of what he calls my son. He's not my son. I've had a power of pleasant times. I recollect once--no I don't--no, it's broken off. It was something about a game of cricket and a friend of mine, but it's somehow broken off. I wonder who he was--I suppose I liked him? And I wonder what became of him--I suppose he died? But I don't know. And I don't care, neither; I don't care a bit."

In his drowsy chuckling, and the shaking of his head, he put his hands into his waistcoat pockets. In one of them he found a bit of holly (left there, probably last night), which he now took out, and looked at.

"Berries, eh?" said the old man. "Ah! It's a pity they're not good to eat. I recollect, when I was a little chap about as high as that, and out a walking with--let me see--who was I out a walking with?--no, I don't remember how that was. I don't remember as I ever walked with any one particular, or cared for any one, or any one for me. Berries, eh? There's good cheer when there's berries. Well; I ought to have my share of it, and to be waited on, and kept warm and comfortable; for I'm eighty-seven, and a poor old man. I'm eigh-ty-seven. Eigh-ty-seven!"

The drivelling, pitiable manner in which, as he repeated this, he nibbled at the leaves, and spat the morsels out; the cold, uninterested eye with which his youngest son (so changed) regarded him; the determined apathy with which his eldest son lay hardened in his sin; impressed themselves no more on Redlaw's observation,-- for he broke his way from the spot to which his feet seemed to have been fixed, and ran out of the house.

His guide came crawling forth from his place of refuge, and was ready for him before he reached the arches.

"Back to the woman's?" he inquired.

"Back, quickly!" answered Redlaw. "Stop nowhere on the way!"

For a short distance the boy went on before; but their return was more like a flight than a walk, and it was as much as his bare feet could do, to keep pace with the Chemist's rapid strides. Shrinking from all who passed, shrouded in his cloak, and keeping it drawn closely about him, as though there were mortal contagion in any fluttering touch of his garments, he made no pause until they reached the door by which they had come out. He unlocked it with his key, went in, accompanied by the boy, and hastened through the dark passages to his own chamber.

The boy watched him as he made the door fast, and withdrew behind the table, when he looked round.

"Come!" he said. "Don't you touch me! You've not brought me here to take my money away."

Redlaw threw some more upon the ground. He flung his body on it immediately, as if to hide it from him, lest the sight of it should tempt him to reclaim it; and not until he saw him seated by his lamp, with his face hidden in his hands, began furtively to pick it up. When he had done so, he crept near the fire, and, sitting down in a great chair before it, took from his breast some broken scraps of food, and fell to munching, and to staring at the blaze, and now and then to glancing at his shillings, which he kept clenched up in a bunch, in one hand.

"And this," said Redlaw, gazing on him with increased repugnance and fear, "is the only one companion I have left on earth!"

How long it was before he was aroused from his contemplation of this creature, whom he dreaded so--whether half-an-hour, or half the night--he knew not. But the stillness of the room was broken by the boy (whom he had seen listening) starting up, and running towards the door.

"Here's the woman coming!" he exclaimed.

The Chemist stopped him on his way, at the moment when she knocked.

"Let me go to her, will you?" said the boy.

"Not now," returned the Chemist. "Stay here. Nobody must pass in or out of the room now. Who's that?"

"It's I, sir," cried Milly. "Pray, sir, let me in!"

"No! not for the world!" he said.

"Mr. Redlaw, Mr. Redlaw, pray, sir, let me in."

"What is the matter?" he said, holding the boy.

"The miserable man you saw, is worse, and nothing I can say will wake him from his terrible infatuation. William's father has turned childish in a moment, William himself is changed. The shock has been too sudden for him; I cannot understand him; he is not like himself. Oh, Mr. Redlaw, pray advise me, help me!"

"No! No! No!" he answered.

"Mr. Redlaw! Dear sir! George has been muttering, in his doze, about the man you saw there, who, he fears, will kill himself."

"Better he should do it, than come near me!"

"He says, in his wandering, that you know him; that he was your friend once, long ago; that he is the ruined father of a student here--my mind misgives me, of the young gentleman who has been ill. What is to be done? How is he to be followed? How is he to be saved? Mr. Redlaw, pray, oh, pray, advise me! Help me!"

All this time he held the boy, who was half-mad to pass him, and let her in.

"Phantoms! Punishers of impious thoughts!" cried Redlaw, gazing round in anguish, "look upon me! From the darkness of my mind, let the glimmering of contrition that I know is there, shine up and show my misery! In the material world as I have long taught, nothing can be spared; no step or atom in the wondrous structure could be lost, without a blank being made in the great universe. I know, now, that it is the same with good and evil, happiness and sorrow, in the memories of men. Pity me! Relieve me!"

There was no response, but her "Help me, help me, let me in!" and the boy's struggling to get to her.

"Shadow of myself! Spirit of my darker hours!" cried Redlaw, in distraction, "come back, and haunt me day and night, but take this gift away! Or, if it must still rest with me, deprive me of the dreadful power of giving it to others. Undo what I have done. Leave me benighted, but restore the day to those whom I have cursed. As I have spared this woman from the first, and as I never will go forth again, but will die here, with no hand to tend me, save this creature's who is proof against me,--hear me!"

The only reply still was, the boy struggling to get to her, while he held him back; and the cry, increasing in its energy, "Help! let me in. He was your friend once, how shall he be followed, how shall he be saved? They are all changed, there is no one else to help me, pray, pray, let me in!"

CHAPTER III--The Gift Reversed

Night was still heavy in the sky. On open plains, from hill-tops, and from the decks of solitary ships at sea, a distant low-lying line, that promised by-and-by to change to light, was visible in the dim horizon; but its promise was remote and doubtful, and the moon was striving with the night-clouds busily.

The shadows upon Redlaw's mind succeeded thick and fast to one another, and obscured its light as the night-clouds hovered between the moon and earth, and kept the latter veiled in darkness. Fitful and uncertain as the shadows which the night-clouds cast, were their concealments from him, and imperfect revelations to him; and, like the night-clouds still, if the clear light broke forth for a moment, it was only that they might sweep over it, and make the darkness deeper than before.

Without, there was a profound and solemn hush upon the ancient pile of building, and its buttresses and angles made dark shapes of mystery upon the ground, which now seemed to retire into the smooth white snow and now seemed to come out of it, as the moon's path was more or less beset. Within, the Chemist's room was indistinct and murky, by the light of the expiring lamp; a ghostly silence had succeeded to the knocking and the voice outside; nothing was audible but, now and then, a low sound among the whitened ashes of the fire, as of its yielding up its last breath. Before it on the ground the boy lay fast asleep. In his chair, the Chemist sat, as he had sat there since the calling at his door had ceased--like a man turned to stone.

At such a time, the Christmas music he had heard before, began to play. He listened to it at first, as he had listened in the church-yard; but presently--it playing still, and being borne towards him on the night air, in a low, sweet, melancholy strain-- he rose, and stood stretching his hands about him, as if there were some friend approaching within his reach, on whom his desolate touch might rest, yet do no harm. As he did this, his face became less fixed and wondering; a gentle trembling came upon him; and at last his eyes filled with tears, and he put his hands before them, and bowed down his head.

His memory of sorrow, wrong, and trouble, had not come back to him; he knew that it was not restored; he had no passing belief or hope that it was. But some dumb stir within him made him capable, again, of being moved by what was hidden, afar off, in the music. If it were only that it told him sorrowfully the value of what he had lost, he thanked Heaven for it with a fervent gratitude.

As the last chord died upon his ear, he raised his head to listen to its lingering vibration. Beyond the boy, so that his sleeping figure lay at its feet, the Phantom stood, immovable and silent, with its eyes upon him.

Ghastly it was, as it had ever been, but not so cruel and relentless in its aspect--or he thought or hoped so, as he looked upon it trembling. It was not alone, but in its shadowy hand it held another hand.

And whose was that? Was the form that stood beside it indeed Milly's, or but her shade and picture? The quiet head was bent a little, as her manner was, and her eyes were looking down, as if in pity, on the sleeping child. A radiant light fell on her face, but did not touch the Phantom; for, though close beside her, it was dark and colourless as ever.

"Spectre!" said the Chemist, newly troubled as he looked, "I have not been stubborn or presumptuous in respect of her. Oh, do not bring her here. Spare me that!"

"This is but a shadow," said the Phantom; "when the morning shines seek out the reality whose image I present before you."

"Is it my inexorable doom to do so?" cried the Chemist.

"It is," replied the Phantom.

"To destroy her peace, her goodness; to make her what I am myself, and what I have made of others!"

"I have said seek her out," returned the Phantom. "I have said no more."

"Oh, tell me," exclaimed Redlaw, catching at the hope which he fancied might lie hidden in the words. "Can I undo what I have done?"

"No," returned the Phantom.

"I do not ask for restoration to myself," said Redlaw. "What I abandoned, I abandoned of my own free will, and have justly lost. But for those to whom I have transferred the fatal gift; who never sought it; who unknowingly received a curse of which they had no warning, and which they had no power to shun; can I do nothing?"

"Nothing," said the Phantom.

"If I cannot, can any one?"

The Phantom, standing like a statue, kept its gaze upon him for a while; then turned its head suddenly, and looked upon the shadow at its side.

"Ah! Can she?" cried Redlaw, still looking upon the shade.

The Phantom released the hand it had retained till now, and softly raised its own with a gesture of dismissal. Upon that, her shadow, still preserving the same attitude, began to move or melt away.

"Stay," cried Redlaw with an earnestness to which he could not give enough expression. "For a moment! As an act of mercy! I know that some change fell upon me, when those sounds were in the air just now. Tell me, have I lost the power of harming her? May I go near her without dread? Oh, let her give me any sign of hope!"

The Phantom looked upon the shade as he did--not at him--and gave no answer.

"At least, say this--has she, henceforth, the consciousness of any power to set right what I have done?"

"She has not," the Phantom answered.

"Has she the power bestowed on her without the consciousness?"

The phantom answered: "Seek her out."

And her shadow slowly vanished.

They were face to face again, and looking on each other, as intently and awfully as at the time of the bestowal of the gift, across the boy who still lay on the ground between them, at the Phantom's feet.

"Terrible instructor," said the Chemist, sinking on his knee before it, in an attitude of supplication, "by whom I was renounced, but by whom I am revisited (in which, and in whose milder aspect, I would fain believe I have a gleam of hope), I will obey without inquiry, praying that the cry I have sent up in the anguish of my soul has been, or will be, heard, in behalf of those whom I have injured beyond human reparation. But there is one thing--"

"You speak to me of what is lying here," the phantom interposed, and pointed with its finger to the boy.

"I do," returned the Chemist. "You know what I would ask. Why has this child alone been proof against my influence, and why, why, have I detected in its thoughts a terrible companionship with mine?"

"This," said the Phantom, pointing to the boy, "is the last, completest illustration of a human creature, utterly bereft of such remembrances as you have yielded up. No softening memory of sorrow, wrong, or trouble enters here, because this wretched mortal from his birth has been abandoned to a worse condition than the beasts, and has, within his knowledge, no one contrast, no humanising touch, to make a grain of such a memory spring up in his hardened breast. All within this desolate creature is barren wilderness. All within the man bereft of what you have resigned, is the same barren wilderness. Woe to such a man! Woe, tenfold, to the nation that shall count its monsters such as this, lying here, by hundreds and by thousands!"

Redlaw shrank, appalled, from what he heard.

"There is not," said the Phantom, "one of these--not one--but sows a harvest that mankind MUST reap. From every seed of evil in this boy, a field of ruin is grown that shall be gathered in, and garnered up, and sown again in many places in the world, until regions are overspread with wickedness enough to raise the waters of another Deluge. Open and unpunished murder in a city's streets would be less guilty in its daily toleration, than one such spectacle as this."

It seemed to look down upon the boy in his sleep. Redlaw, too, looked down upon him with a new emotion.

"There is not a father," said the Phantom, "by whose side in his daily or his nightly walk, these creatures pass; there is not a mother among all the ranks of loving mothers in this land; there is no one risen from the state of childhood, but shall be responsible in his or her degree for this enormity. There is not a country throughout the earth on which it would not bring a curse. There is no religion upon earth that it would not deny; there is no people upon earth it would not put to shame."

The Chemist clasped his hands, and looked, with trembling fear and pity, from the sleeping boy to the Phantom, standing above him with his finger pointing down.

"Behold, I say," pursued the Spectre, "the perfect type of what it was your choice to be. Your influence is powerless here, because from this child's bosom you can banish nothing. His thoughts have been in 'terrible companionship' with yours, because you have gone down to his unnatural level. He is the growth of man's indifference; you are the growth of man's presumption. The beneficent design of Heaven is, in each case, overthrown, and from the two poles of the immaterial world you come together."

The Chemist stooped upon the ground beside the boy, and, with the same kind of compassion for him that he now felt for himself, covered him as he slept, and no longer shrank from him with abhorrence or indifference.

Soon, now, the distant line on the horizon brightened, the darkness faded, the sun rose red and glorious, and the chimney stacks and gables of the ancient building gleamed in the clear air, which turned the smoke and vapour of the city into a cloud of gold. The very sun-dial in his shady corner, where the wind was used to spin with such unwindy constancy, shook off the finer particles of snow that had accumulated on his dull old face in the night, and looked out at the little white wreaths eddying round and round him. Doubtless some blind groping of the morning made its way down into the forgotten crypt so cold and earthy, where the Norman arches were half buried in the ground, and stirred the dull sap in the lazy vegetation hanging to the walls, and quickened the slow principle of life within the little world of wonderful and delicate creation which existed there, with some faint knowledge that the sun was up.

The Tetterbys were up, and doing. Mr. Tetterby took down the shutters of the shop, and, strip by strip, revealed the treasures of the window to the eyes, so proof against their seductions, of Jerusalem Buildings. Adolphus had been out so long already, that he was halfway on to "Morning Pepper." Five small Tetterbys, whose ten round eyes were much inflamed by soap and friction, were in the tortures of a cool wash in the back kitchen; Mrs. Tetterby presiding. Johnny, who was pushed and hustled through his toilet with great rapidity when Moloch chanced to be in an exacting frame of mind (which was always the case), staggered up and down with his charge before the shop door, under greater difficulties than usual; the weight of Moloch being much increased by a complication of defences against the cold, composed of knitted worsted-work, and forming a complete suit of chain-armour, with a head-piece and blue gaiters.

It was a peculiarity of this baby to be always cutting teeth. Whether they never came, or whether they came and went away again, is not in evidence; but it had certainly cut enough, on the showing of Mrs. Tetterby, to make a handsome dental provision for the sign of the Bull and Mouth. All sorts of objects were impressed for the rubbing of its gums, notwithstanding that it always carried, dangling at its waist (which was immediately under its chin), a bone ring, large enough to have represented the rosary of a young nun. Knife-handles, umbrella-tops, the heads of walking-sticks selected from the stock, the fingers of the family in general, but especially of Johnny, nutmeg-graters, crusts, the handles of doors, and the cool knobs on the tops of pokers, were among the commonest instruments indiscriminately applied for this baby's relief. The amount of electricity that must have been rubbed out of it in a week, is not to be calculated. Still Mrs. Tetterby always said "it was coming through, and then the child would be herself;" and still it never did come through, and the child continued to be somebody else.

The tempers of the little Tetterbys had sadly changed with a few hours. Mr. and Mrs. Tetterby themselves were not more altered than their offspring. Usually they were an unselfish, good-natured, yielding little race, sharing short commons when it happened (which was pretty often) contentedly and even generously, and taking a great deal of enjoyment out of a very little meat. But they were fighting now, not only for the soap and water, but even for the breakfast which was yet in perspective. The hand of every little Tetterby was against the other little Tetterbys; and even Johnny's hand--the patient, much-enduring, and devoted Johnny--rose against the baby! Yes, Mrs. Tetterby, going to the door by mere accident, saw him viciously pick out a weak place in the suit of armour where a slap would tell, and slap that blessed child.

Mrs. Tetterby had him into the parlour by the collar, in that same flash of time, and repaid him the assault with usury thereto.

"You brute, you murdering little boy," said Mrs. Tetterby. "Had you the heart to do it?"

"Why don't her teeth come through, then," retorted Johnny, in a loud rebellious voice, "instead of bothering me? How would you like it yourself?"

"Like it, sir!" said Mrs. Tetterby, relieving him of his dishonoured load.

"Yes, like it," said Johnny. "How would you? Not at all. If you was me, you'd go for a soldier. I will, too. There an't no babies in the Army."

Mr. Tetterby, who had arrived upon the scene of action, rubbed his chin thoughtfully, instead of correcting the rebel, and seemed rather struck by this view of a military life.

"I wish I was in the Army myself, if the child's in the right," said Mrs. Tetterby, looking at her husband, "for I have no peace of my life here. I'm a slave--a Virginia slave:" some indistinct association with their weak descent on the tobacco trade perhaps suggested this aggravated expression to Mrs. Tetterby. "I never have a holiday, or any pleasure at all, from year's end to year's end! Why, Lord bless and save the child," said Mrs. Tetterby, shaking the baby with an irritability hardly suited to so pious an aspiration, "what's the matter with her now?"

Not being able to discover, and not rendering the subject much clearer by shaking it, Mrs. Tetterby put the baby away in a cradle, and, folding her arms, sat rocking it angrily with her foot.

"How you stand there, 'Dolphus," said Mrs. Tetterby to her husband. "Why don't you do something?"

"Because I don't care about doing anything," Mr. Tetterby replied.

"I am sure *I* don't," said Mrs. Tetterby.

"I'll take my oath *I* don't," said Mr. Tetterby.

A diversion arose here among Johnny and his five younger brothers, who, in preparing the family breakfast table, had fallen to skirmishing for the temporary possession of the loaf, and were buffeting one another with great heartiness; the smallest boy of all, with precocious discretion, hovering outside the knot of combatants, and harassing their legs. Into the midst of this fray, Mr. and Mrs. Tetterby both precipitated themselves with great ardour, as if such ground were the only ground on which they could now agree; and having, with no visible remains of their late soft- heartedness, laid about them without any lenity, and done much execution, resumed their former relative positions.

"You had better read your paper than do nothing at all," said Mrs. Tetterby.

"What's there to read in a paper?" returned Mr. Tetterby, with excessive discontent.

"What?" said Mrs. Tetterby. "Police."

"It's nothing to me," said Tetterby. "What do I care what people do, or are done to?"

"Suicides," suggested Mrs. Tetterby.

"No business of mine," replied her husband.

"Births, deaths, and marriages, are those nothing to you?" said Mrs. Tetterby.

"If the births were all over for good, and all to-day; and the deaths were all to begin to come off to-morrow; I don't see why it should interest me, till I thought it was a coming to my turn," grumbled Tetterby. "As to marriages, I've done it myself. I know quite enough about THEM."

To judge from the dissatisfied expression of her face and manner, Mrs. Tetterby appeared to entertain the same opinions as her husband; but she opposed him, nevertheless, for the gratification of quarrelling with him.

"Oh, you're a consistent man," said Mrs. Tetterby, "an't you? You, with the screen of your own making there, made of nothing else but bits of newspapers, which you sit and read to the children by the half-hour together!"

"Say used to, if you please," returned her husband. "You won't find me doing so any more. I'm wiser now."

"Bah! wiser, indeed!" said Mrs. Tetterby. "Are you better?"

The question sounded some discordant note in Mr. Tetterby's breast. He ruminated dejectedly, and passed his hand across and across his forehead.

"Better!" murmured Mr. Tetterby. "I don't know as any of us are better, or happier either. Better, is it?"

He turned to the screen, and traced about it with his finger, until he found a certain paragraph of which he was in quest.

"This used to be one of the family favourites, I recollect," said Tetterby, in a forlorn and stupid way, "and used to draw tears from the children, and make 'em good, if there was any little bickering or discontent among 'em, next to the story of the robin redbreasts in the wood. 'Melancholy case of destitution. Yesterday a small man, with a baby in his arms, and surrounded by half-a-dozen ragged little ones, of various ages between ten and two, the whole of whom were evidently in a famishing condition, appeared before the worthy magistrate, and made the following recital:'--Ha! I don't understand it, I'm sure," said Tetterby; "I don't see what it has got to do with us."

"How old and shabby he looks," said Mrs. Tetterby, watching him. "I never saw such a change in a man. Ah! dear me, dear me, dear me, it was a sacrifice!"

"What was a sacrifice?" her husband sourly inquired.

Mrs. Tetterby shook her head; and without replying in words, raised a complete sea-storm about the baby, by her violent agitation of the cradle.

"If you mean your marriage was a sacrifice, my good woman--" said her husband.

"I DO mean it" said his wife.

"Why, then I mean to say," pursued Mr. Tetterby, as sulkily and surlily as she, "that there are two sides to that affair; and that I was the sacrifice; and that I wish the sacrifice hadn't been accepted."

"I wish it hadn't, Tetterby, with all my heart and soul I do assure you," said his wife. "You can't wish it more than I do, Tetterby."

"I don't know what I saw in her," muttered the newsman, "I'm sure;- -certainly, if I saw anything, it's not there now. I was thinking so, last night, after supper, by the fire. She's fat, she's ageing, she won't bear comparison with most other women."

"He's common-looking, he has no air with him, he's small, he's beginning to stoop and he's getting bald," muttered Mrs. Tetterby.

"I must have been half out of my mind when I did it," muttered Mr. Tetterby.

"My senses must have forsook me. That's the only way in which I can explain it to myself," said Mrs. Tetterby with elaboration.

In this mood they sat down to breakfast. The little Tetterbys were not habituated to regard that meal in the light of a sedentary occupation, but discussed it as a dance or trot; rather resembling a savage ceremony, in the occasionally shrill whoops, and brandishings of bread and butter, with which it was accompanied, as well as in the intricate filings off into the street and back again, and the hoppings up and down the door-steps, which were incidental to the performance. In the present instance, the contentions between these Tetterby children for the milk-

and-water jug, common to all, which stood upon the table, presented so lamentable an instance of angry passions risen very high indeed, that it was an outrage on the memory of Dr. Watts. It was not until Mr. Tetterby had driven the whole herd out at the front door, that a moment's peace was secured; and even that was broken by the discovery that Johnny had surreptitiously come back, and was at that instant choking in the jug like a ventriloquist, in his indecent and rapacious haste.

"These children will be the death of me at last!" said Mrs. Tetterby, after banishing the culprit. "And the sooner the better, I think."

"Poor people," said Mr. Tetterby, "ought not to have children at all. They give US no pleasure."

He was at that moment taking up the cup which Mrs. Tetterby had rudely pushed towards him, and Mrs. Tetterby was lifting her own cup to her lips, when they both stopped, as if they were transfixed.

"Here! Mother! Father!" cried Johnny, running into the room. "Here's Mrs. William coming down the street!"

And if ever, since the world began, a young boy took a baby from a cradle with the care of an old nurse, and hushed and soothed it tenderly, and tottered away with it cheerfully, Johnny was that boy, and Moloch was that baby, as they went out together!

Mr. Tetterby put down his cup; Mrs. Tetterby put down her cup. Mr. Tetterby rubbed his forehead; Mrs. Tetterby rubbed hers. Mr. Tetterby's face began to smooth and brighten; Mrs. Tetterby's began to smooth and brighten.

"Why, Lord forgive me," said Mr. Tetterby to himself, "what evil tempers have I been giving way to? What has been the matter here!"

"How could I ever treat him ill again, after all I said and felt last night!" sobbed Mrs. Tetterby, with her apron to her eyes.

"Am I a brute," said Mr. Tetterby, "or is there any good in me at all? Sophia! My little woman!"

"'Dolphus dear," returned his wife.

"I--I've been in a state of mind," said Mr. Tetterby, "that I can't abear to think of, Sophy."

"Oh! It's nothing to what I've been in, Dolf," cried his wife in a great burst of grief.

"My Sophia," said Mr. Tetterby, "don't take on. I never shall forgive myself. I must have nearly broke your heart, I know."

"No, Dolf, no. It was me! Me!" cried Mrs. Tetterby.

"My little woman," said her husband, "don't. You make me reproach myself dreadful, when you show such a noble spirit. Sophia, my dear, you don't know what I thought. I showed it bad enough, no doubt; but what I thought, my little woman!--"

"Oh, dear Dolf, don't! Don't!" cried his wife.

"Sophia," said Mr. Tetterby, "I must reveal it. I couldn't rest in my conscience unless I mentioned it. My little woman--"

"Mrs. William's very nearly here!" screamed Johnny at the door.

"My little woman, I wondered how," gasped Mr. Tetterby, supporting himself by his chair, "I wondered how I had ever admired you--I forgot the precious children you have brought about me, and thought you didn't look as slim as I could wish. I--I never gave a recollection," said Mr. Tetterby, with severe self-accusation, "to the cares you've had as my wife, and along of me and mine, when you might have had hardly any with another man, who got on better and was luckier than me (anybody might have found such a man easily I am sure); and I quarrelled with you for having aged a little in the rough years you have lightened for me. Can you believe it, my little woman? I hardly can myself."

Mrs. Tetterby, in a whirlwind of laughing and crying, caught his face within her hands, and held it there.

"Oh, Dolf!" she cried. "I am so happy that you thought so; I am so grateful that you thought so! For I thought that you were common- looking, Dolf; and so you are, my dear, and may you be the commonest of all sights in my eyes, till you close them with your own good hands. I thought that you were small; and so you are, and I'll make much of you because you are, and more of you because I love my husband. I thought that you began to stoop; and so you do, and you shall lean on me, and I'll do all I can to keep you up. I thought there was no air about you; but there is, and it's the air of home, and that's the purest and the best there is, and God bless home once more, and all belonging to it, Dolf!"

"Hurrah! Here's Mrs. William!" cried Johnny.

So she was, and all the children with her; and so she came in, they kissed her, and kissed one another, and kissed the baby, and kissed their father and mother, and then ran back and flocked and danced about her, trooping on with her in triumph.

Mr. and Mrs. Tetterby were not a bit behind-hand in the warmth of their reception. They were as much attracted to her as the children were; they ran towards her, kissed her hands, pressed round her, could not receive her ardently or enthusiastically enough. She came among them like the spirit of all goodness, affection, gentle consideration, love, and domesticity.

"What! are YOU all so glad to see me, too, this bright Christmas morning?" said Milly, clapping her hands in a pleasant wonder. "Oh dear, how delightful this is!"

More shouting from the children, more kissing, more trooping round her, more happiness, more love, more joy, more honour, on all sides, than she could bear.

"Oh dear!" said Milly, "what delicious tears you make me shed. How can I ever have deserved this! What have I done to be so loved?"

"Who can help it!" cried Mr. Tetterby.

"Who can help it!" cried Mrs. Tetterby.

"Who can help it!" echoed the children, in a joyful chorus. And they danced and trooped about her again, and clung to her, and laid their rosy faces against her dress, and kissed and fondled it, and could not fondle it, or her, enough.

"I never was so moved," said Milly, drying her eyes, "as I have been this morning. I must tell you, as soon as I can speak.--Mr. Redlaw came to me at sunrise, and with a tenderness in his manner, more as if I had been his darling daughter than myself, implored me to go with him to where William's brother George is lying ill. We went together, and all the way along he was so kind, and so subdued, and seemed to put such trust and hope in me, that I could not help trying with pleasure. When we got to the house, we met a woman at the door (somebody had bruised and hurt her, I am afraid), who caught me by the hand, and blessed me as I passed."

"She was right!" said Mr. Tetterby. Mrs. Tetterby said she was right. All the children cried out that she was right.

"Ah, but there's more than that," said Milly. "When we got up stairs, into the room, the sick man who had lain for hours in a state from which no effort could rouse him, rose up in his bed, and, bursting into tears, stretched out his arms to me, and said that he had led a mis-spent life, but that he was truly repentant now, in his sorrow for the past, which was all as plain to him as a great prospect, from which a dense black cloud had cleared away, and that he entreated me to ask his poor old father for his pardon and his blessing, and to say a prayer beside his bed. And when I did so, Mr. Redlaw joined in it so fervently, and then so thanked and thanked me, and thanked Heaven, that my heart quite overflowed, and I could have done nothing but sob and cry, if the sick man had not begged me to sit down by him,--which made me quiet of course. As I sat there, he held my hand in his until he sank in a doze; and even then, when I withdrew my hand to leave him to come here (which Mr. Redlaw was very earnest indeed in wishing me to do), his hand felt for mine, so that some one else was obliged to take my place and make believe to give him my hand back. Oh dear, oh dear," said Milly, sobbing. "How thankful and how happy I should feel, and do feel, for all this!"

While she was speaking, Redlaw had come in, and, after pausing for a moment to observe the group of which she was the centre, had silently ascended the stairs. Upon those stairs he now appeared again; remaining there, while the young student passed him, and came running down.

"Kind nurse, gentlest, best of creatures," he said, falling on his knee to her, and catching at her hand, "forgive my cruel ingratitude!"

"Oh dear, oh dear!" cried Milly innocently, "here's another of them! Oh dear, here's somebody else who likes me. What shall I ever do!"

The guileless, simple way in which she said it, and in which she put her hands before her eyes and wept for very happiness, was as touching as it was delightful.

"I was not myself," he said. "I don't know what it was--it was some consequence of my disorder perhaps--I was mad. But I am so no longer. Almost as I speak, I am restored. I heard the children crying out your name, and the shade passed from me at the very sound of it. Oh, don't weep! Dear Milly, if you could read my heart, and only knew with what affection and what grateful homage it is glowing, you would not let me see you weep. It is such deep reproach."

"No, no," said Milly, "it's not that. It's not indeed. It's joy. It's wonder that you should think it necessary to ask me to forgive so little, and yet it's pleasure that you do."

"And will you come again? and will you finish the little curtain?"

"No," said Milly, drying her eyes, and shaking her head. "You won't care for my needlework now."

"Is it forgiving me, to say that?"

She beckoned him aside, and whispered in his ear.

"There is news from your home, Mr. Edmund."

"News? How?"

"Either your not writing when you were very ill, or the change in your hand-writing when you began to be better, created some suspicion of the truth; however that is--but you're sure you'll not be the worse for any news, if it's not bad news?"

"Sure."

"Then there's some one come!" said Milly.

"My mother?" asked the student, glancing round involuntarily towards Red-law, who had come down from the stairs.

"Hush! No," said Milly.

"It can be no one else."

"Indeed?" said Milly, "are you sure?"

"It is not -" Before he could say more, she put her hand upon his mouth.

"Yes it is!" said Milly. "The young lady (she is very like the miniature, Mr. Edmund, but she is prettier) was too unhappy to rest without satisfying her doubts, and came up, last night, with a little servant-maid. As you always dated your letters from the college, she came there; and before I saw Mr. Redlaw this morning, I saw her. SHE likes me too!" said Milly. "Oh dear, that's another!"

"This morning! Where is she now?"

"Why, she is now," said Milly, advancing her lips to his ear, "in my little par-lour in the Lodge, and waiting to see you."

He pressed her hand, and was darting off, but she detained him.

"Mr. Redlaw is much altered, and has told me this morning that his memory is impaired. Be very considerate to him, Mr. Edmund; he needs that from us all."

The young man assured her, by a look, that her caution was not ill- bestowed; and as he passed the Chemist on his way out, bent respectfully and with an obvious interest before him.

Redlaw returned the salutation courteously and even humbly, and looked after him as he passed on. He dropped his head upon his hand too, as trying to reawaken something he had lost. But it was gone.

The abiding change that had come upon him since the influence of the music, and the Phantom's reappearance, was, that now he truly felt how much he had lost, and could compassionate his own condition, and contrast it, clearly, with the natural state of those who were around him. In this, an interest in those who were around him was revived, and a meek, submissive sense of his calamity was bred, resembling that which sometimes obtains in age, when its mental powers are weakened, without insensibility or sullenness being added to the list of its infirmities.

He was conscious that, as he redeemed, through Milly, more and more of the evil he had done, and as he was more and more with her, this change ripened itself within him. Therefore, and because of the attachment she inspired him with (but without other hope), he felt that he was quite dependent on her, and that she was his staff in his affliction.

So, when she asked him whether they should go home now, to where the old man and her husband were, and he readily replied "yes"-- being anxious in that regard--he put his arm through hers, and walked beside her; not as if he were the wise and learned man to whom the wonders of Nature were an open book, and hers were the uninstructed mind, but as if their two positions were reversed, and he knew nothing, and she all.

He saw the children throng about her, and caress her, as he and she went away together thus, out of the house; he heard the ringing of their laughter, and their merry voices; he saw their bright faces, clustering around him like flowers; he witnessed the renewed contentment and affection of their parents; he breathed the simple air of their poor home, restored to its tranquillity; he thought of the unwholesome blight he had shed upon it, and might, but for her, have been diffusing then; and perhaps it is no wonder that he walked submissively beside her, and drew her gentle bosom nearer to his own.

When they arrived at the Lodge, the old man was sitting in his chair in the chimney-corner, with his eyes fixed on the ground, and his son was leaning against the opposite side of the fire-place, looking at him. As she came in at the door, both started, and turned round towards her, and a radiant change came upon their faces.

"Oh dear, dear, dear, they are all pleased to see me like the rest!" cried Milly, clapping her hands in an ecstasy, and stopping short. "Here are two more!"

Pleased to see her! Pleasure was no word for it. She ran into her husband's arms, thrown wide open to receive her, and he would have been glad to have her there, with her head lying on his shoulder, through the short winter's day. But the old man couldn't spare her. He had arms for her too, and he locked her in them.

"Why, where has my quiet Mouse been all this time?" said the old man. "She has been a long while away. I find that it's impossible for me to get on without Mouse. I--where's my son William?--I fancy I have been dreaming, William."

"That's what I say myself, father," returned his son. "I have been in an ugly sort of dream, I think.--How are you, father? Are you pretty well?"

"Strong and brave, my boy," returned the old man.

It was quite a sight to see Mr. William shaking hands with his father, and patting him on the back, and rubbing him gently down with his hand, as if he could not possibly do enough to show an interest in him.

"What a wonderful man you are, father!--How are you, father? Are you really pretty hearty, though?" said William, shaking hands with him again, and patting him again, and rubbing him gently down again.

"I never was fresher or stouter in my life, my boy."

"What a wonderful man you are, father! But that's exactly where it is," said Mr. William, with enthusiasm. "When I think of all that my father's gone through, and all the chances and changes, and sorrows and troubles, that have happened to him in the course of his long life, and under which his head has grown grey, and years upon years have gathered on it, I feel as if we couldn't do enough to honour the old gentleman, and make his old age easy.--How are you, father? Are you really pretty well, though?"

Mr. William might never have left off repeating this inquiry, and shaking hands with him again, and patting him again, and rubbing him down again, if the old man had not espied the Chemist, whom until now he had not seen.

"I ask your pardon, Mr. Redlaw," said Philip, "but didn't know you were here, sir, or should have made less free. It reminds me, Mr. Redlaw, seeing you here on a Christmas morning, of the time when you was a student yourself, and worked so hard that you were backwards and forwards in our Library even at Christmas time. Ha! ha! I'm old enough to remember that; and I remember it right well, I do, though I am eight-seven. It was after you left here that my poor wife died. You remember my poor wife, Mr. Redlaw?"

The Chemist answered yes.

"Yes," said the old man. "She was a dear creetur.--I recollect you come here one Christmas morning with a young lady--I ask your pardon, Mr. Redlaw, but I think it was a sister you was very much attached to?"

The Chemist looked at him, and shook his head. "I had a sister," he said vacantly. He knew no more.

"One Christmas morning," pursued the old man, "that you come here with her--and it began to snow, and my wife invited the lady to walk in, and sit by the fire that is always a burning on Christmas Day in what used to be, before our ten poor gentlemen commuted, our great Dinner Hall. I was there; and I recollect, as I was stirring up the blaze for the young lady to warm her pretty feet by, she read the scroll out loud, that is underneath that pictur, 'Lord, keep my memory green!' She and my poor wife fell a talking about it; and it's a strange thing to think of, now, that they both said (both being so unlike to die) that it was a good prayer, and that it was one they would put up very earnestly, if they were called away young, with reference to those who were dearest to them. 'My brother,' says the young lady--'My husband,' says my poor wife.-- 'Lord, keep his memory of me, green, and do not let me be forgotten!'"

Tears more painful, and more bitter than he had ever shed in all his life, coursed down Redlaw's face. Philip, fully occupied in recalling his story, had not observed him until now, nor Milly's anxiety that he should not proceed.

"Philip!" said Redlaw, laying his hand upon his arm, "I am a stricken man, on whom the hand of Providence has fallen heavily, although deservedly. You speak to me, my friend, of what I cannot follow; my memory is gone."

"Merciful power!" cried the old man.

"I have lost my memory of sorrow, wrong, and trouble," said the Chemist, "and with that I have lost all man would remember!"

To see old Philip's pity for him, to see him wheel his own great chair for him to rest in, and look down upon him with a solemn sense of his bereavement, was to know, in some degree, how precious to old age such recollections are.

The boy came running in, and ran to Milly.

"Here's the man," he said, "in the other room. I don't want HIM."

"What man does he mean?" asked Mr. William.

"Hush!" said Milly.

Obedient to a sign from her, he and his old father softly withdrew. As they went out, unnoticed, Redlaw beckoned to the boy to come to him.

"I like the woman best," he answered, holding to her skirts.

"You are right," said Redlaw, with a faint smile. "But you needn't fear to come to me. I am gentler than I was. Of all the world, to you, poor child!"

The boy still held back at first, but yielding little by little to her urging, he consented to approach, and even to sit down at his feet. As Redlaw laid his hand upon the shoulder of the child, looking on him with compassion and a fellow-feeling, he put out his other hand to Milly. She stooped down on that side of him, so that she could look into his face, and after silence, said:

"Mr. Redlaw, may I speak to you?"

"Yes," he answered, fixing his eyes upon her. "Your voice and music are the same to me."

"May I ask you something?"

"What you will."

"Do you remember what I said, when I knocked at your door last night? About one who was your friend once, and who stood on the verge of destruction?"

"Yes. I remember," he said, with some hesitation.

"Do you understand it?"

He smoothed the boy's hair--looking at her fixedly the while, and shook his head.

"This person," said Milly, in her clear, soft voice, which her mild eyes, looking at him, made clearer and softer, "I found soon afterwards. I went back to the house, and, with Heaven's help, traced him. I was not too soon. A very little and I should have been too late."

He took his hand from the boy, and laying it on the back of that hand of hers, whose timid and yet earnest touch addressed him no less appealingly than her voice and eyes, looked more intently on her.

"He IS the father of Mr. Edmund, the young gentleman we saw just now. His real name is Longford.--You recollect the name?"

"I recollect the name."

"And the man?"

"No, not the man. Did he ever wrong me?"

"Yes!"

"Ah! Then it's hopeless--hopeless."

He shook his head, and softly beat upon the hand he held, as though mutely asking her commiseration.

"I did not go to Mr. Edmund last night," said Milly,--"You will listen to me just the same as if you did remember all?"

"To every syllable you say."

"Both, because I did not know, then, that this really was his father, and because I was fearful of the effect of such intelligence upon him, after his illness, if it should be. Since I have known who this person is, I have not gone either; but that is for another reason. He has long been separated from his wife and son--has been a stranger to his home almost from this son's infancy, I learn from him--and has abandoned and deserted what he should have held most dear. In all that time he has been falling from the state of a gentleman, more and more, until--" she rose up, hastily, and going out for a moment, returned, accompanied by the wreck that Redlaw had beheld last night.

"Do you know me?" asked the Chemist.

"I should be glad," returned the other, "and that is an unwonted word for me to use, if I could answer no."

The Chemist looked at the man, standing in self-abasement and degradation before him, and would have looked longer, in an ineffectual struggle for enlightenment, but that Milly resumed her late position by his side, and attracted his attentive gaze to her own face.

"See how low he is sunk, how lost he is!" she whispered, stretching out her arm towards him, without looking from the Chemist's face. "If you could remember all that is connected with him, do you not think it would move your pity to reflect that one you ever loved (do not let us mind how long ago, or in what belief that he has forfeited), should come to this?"

"I hope it would," he answered. "I believe it would."

His eyes wandered to the figure standing near the door, but came back speedily to her, on whom he gazed intently, as if he strove to learn some lesson from every tone of her voice, and every beam of her eyes.

"I have no learning, and you have much," said Milly; "I am not used to think, and you are always thinking. May I tell you why it seems to me a good thing for us, to remember wrong that has been done us?"

"Yes."

"That we may forgive it."

"Pardon me, great Heaven!" said Redlaw, lifting up his eyes, "for having thrown away thine own high attribute!"

"And if," said Milly, "if your memory should one day be restored, as we will hope and pray it may be, would it not be a blessing to you to recall at once a wrong and its forgiveness?"

He looked at the figure by the door, and fastened his attentive eyes on her again; a ray of clearer light appeared to him to shine into his mind, from her bright face.

"He cannot go to his abandoned home. He does not seek to go there. He knows that he could only carry shame and trouble to those he has so cruelly neglected; and that the best reparation he can make them now, is to avoid them. A very little money carefully bestowed, would remove him to some distant place, where he might live and do no wrong, and make such atonement as is left within his power for the wrong he has done. To the unfortunate lady who is his wife, and to his son, this would be the best and kindest boon that their best friend could give them--one too that they need never know of; and to him, shattered in reputation, mind, and body, it might be salvation."

He took her head between her hands, and kissed it, and said: "It shall be done. I trust to you to do it for me, now and secretly; and to tell him that I would forgive him, if I were so happy as to know for what."

As she rose, and turned her beaming face towards the fallen man, implying that her mediation had been successful, he advanced a step, and without raising his eyes, addressed himself to Redlaw.

"You are so generous," he said, "--you ever were--that you will try to banish your rising sense of retribution in the spectacle that is before you. I do not try to banish it from myself, Redlaw. If you can, believe me."

The Chemist entreated Milly, by a gesture, to come nearer to him; and, as he listened looked in her face, as if to find in it the clue to what he heard.

"I am too decayed a wretch to make professions; I recollect my own career too well, to array any such before you. But from the day on which I made my first step downward, in dealing falsely by you, I have gone down with a certain, steady, doomed progression. That, I say."

Redlaw, keeping her close at his side, turned his face towards the speaker, and there was sorrow in it. Something like mournful recognition too.

"I might have been another man, my life might have been another life, if I had avoided that first fatal step. I don't know that it would have been. I claim nothing for the possibility. Your sister is at rest, and better than she could have been with me, if I had continued even what you thought me: even what I once supposed my-self to be."

Redlaw made a hasty motion with his hand, as if he would have put that sub-ject on one side.

"I speak," the other went on, "like a man taken from the grave. I should have made my own grave, last night, had it not been for this blessed hand."

"Oh dear, he likes me too!" sobbed Milly, under her breath. "That's another!"

"I could not have put myself in your way, last night, even for bread. But, to-day, my recollection of what has been is so strongly stirred, and is presented to me, I don't know how, so vividly, that I have dared to come at her suggestion, and to take your bounty, and to thank you for it, and to beg you, Redlaw, in your dying hour, to be as merciful to me in your thoughts, as you are in your deeds."

He turned towards the door, and stopped a moment on his way forth.

"I hope my son may interest you, for his mother's sake. I hope he may deserve to do so. Unless my life should be preserved a long time, and I should know that I have not misused your aid, I shall never look upon him more."

Going out, he raised his eyes to Redlaw for the first time. Redlaw, whose stead-fast gaze was fixed upon him, dreamily held out his hand. He returned and touched it--little more--with both his own; and bending down his head, went slowly out.

In the few moments that elapsed, while Milly silently took him to the gate, the Chemist dropped into his chair, and covered his face with his hands. Seeing him thus, when she came back, accompanied by her husband and his father (who were both greatly concerned for him), she avoided disturbing him, or permitting him to be disturbed; and kneeled down near the chair to put some warm clothing on the boy.

"That's exactly where it is. That's what I always say, father!" exclaimed her admiring husband. "There's a motherly feeling in Mrs. William's breast that must and will have went!"

"Ay, ay," said the old man; "you're right. My son William's right!"

"It happens all for the best, Milly dear, no doubt," said Mr. William, tenderly, "that we have no children of our own; and yet I sometimes wish you had one to love and cherish. Our little dead child that you built such hopes upon, and that never breathed the breath of life--it has made you quiet-like, Milly."

"I am very happy in the recollection of it, William dear," she answered. "I think of it every day."

"I was afraid you thought of it a good deal."

"Don't say, afraid; it is a comfort to me; it speaks to me in so many ways. The innocent thing that never lived on earth, is like an angel to me, William."

"You are like an angel to father and me," said Mr. William, softly. "I know that."

"When I think of all those hopes I built upon it, and the many times I sat and pictured to myself the little smiling face upon my bosom that never lay there, and the sweet eyes turned up to mine that never opened to the light," said Milly, "I can feel a greater tenderness, I think, for all the disappointed hopes in which there is no harm. When I see a beautiful child in its fond mother's arms, I love it all the better, thinking that my child might have been like that, and might have made my heart as proud and happy."

Redlaw raised his head, and looked towards her.

"All through life, it seems by me," she continued, "to tell me something. For poor neglected children, my little child pleads as if it were alive, and had a voice I knew, with which to speak to me. When I hear of youth in suffering or shame, I think that my child might have come to that, perhaps, and that God took it from me in His mercy. Even in age and grey hair, such as father's, it is present: saying that it too might have lived to be old, long and long after you and I were gone, and to have needed the respect and love of younger people."

Her quiet voice was quieter than ever, as she took her husband's arm, and laid her head against it.

"Children love me so, that sometimes I half fancy--it's a silly fancy, William--they have some way I don't know of, of feeling for my little child, and me, and understanding why their love is precious to me. If I have been quiet since, I have been more happy, William, in a hundred ways. Not least happy, dear, in this--that even when my little child was born and dead but a few days, and I was weak and sorrowful, and could not help grieving a little, the thought arose, that if I tried to lead a good life, I should meet in Heaven a bright creature, who would call me, Mother!"

Redlaw fell upon his knees, with a loud cry.

"O Thou, he said, "who through the teaching of pure love, hast graciously restored me to the memory which was the memory of Christ upon the Cross, and of all the good who perished in His cause, receive my thanks, and bless her!"

Then, he folded her to his heart; and Milly, sobbing more than ever, cried, as she laughed, "He is come back to himself! He likes me very much indeed, too! Oh, dear, dear, dear me, here's another!"

Then, the student entered, leading by the hand a lovely girl, who was afraid to come. And Redlaw so changed towards him, seeing in him and his youthful choice, the softened shadow of that chastening passage in his own life, to which, as to a shady tree, the dove so long imprisoned in his solitary ark might fly for rest and company, fell upon his neck, entreating them to be his children.

Then, as Christmas is a time in which, of all times in the year, the memory of every remediable sorrow, wrong, and trouble in the world around us, should be active with us, not less than our own experiences, for all good, he laid his hand upon the boy, and, silently calling Him to witness who laid His hand on children in old time, rebuking, in the majesty of His prophetic knowledge, those who kept them from Him, vowed to protect him, teach him, and reclaim him.

Then, he gave his right hand cheerily to Philip, and said that they would that day hold a Christmas dinner in what used to be, before the ten poor gentlemen commuted, their great Dinner Hall; and that they would bid to it as many of that Swidger family, who, his son had told him, were so numerous that they might join hands and make a ring round England, as could be brought together on so short a notice.

And it was that day done. There were so many Swidgers there, grown up and children, that an attempt to state them in round numbers might engender doubts, in the distrustful, of the veracity of this history. Therefore the attempt shall not be made. But there they were, by dozens and scores--and there was good news and good hope there, ready for them, of George, who had been visited again by his father and brother, and by Milly, and again left in a quiet sleep. There, present at the dinner, too, were the Tetterbys, including young Adolphus, who arrived in his prismatic comforter, in good time for the beef. Johnny and the baby were too late, of course, and came in all on one side, the one exhausted, the other in a supposed state of double-tooth; but that was customary, and not alarming.

It was sad to see the child who had no name or lineage, watching the other children as they played, not knowing how to talk with them, or sport with them, and more strange to the ways of childhood than a rough dog. It was sad, though in a different way, to see what an instinctive knowledge the youngest children there had of his being different from all the rest, and how they made timid approaches to him with soft words and touches, and with little presents, that he might not be unhappy. But he kept by Milly, and began to love her--that was another, as she said!--and, as they all liked her dearly, they were glad of that, and when they saw him peeping at them from behind her chair, they were pleased that he was so close to it.

All this, the Chemist, sitting with the student and his bride that was to be, Philip, and the rest, saw.

Some people have said since, that he only thought what has been herein set down; others, that he read it in the fire, one winter night about the twilight time; others, that the Ghost was but the representation of his gloomy thoughts, and Milly the embodiment of his better wisdom. *I* say nothing.

- Except this. That as they were assembled in the old Hall, by no other light than that of a great fire (having dined early), the shadows once more stole out of their hiding-places, and danced about the room, showing the children marvellous shapes and faces on the walls, and gradually changing what was real and familiar there, to what was wild and magical. But that there was one thing in the Hall, to which the eyes of Redlaw, and of Milly and her husband, and of the old man, and of the student, and his bride that was to be, were often turned, which the shadows did not obscure or change. Deepened in its gravity by the fire-light, and gazing from the darkness of the panelled wall like life, the sedate face in the portrait, with the beard and ruff, looked down at them from under its verdant wreath of holly, as they looked up at it; and, clear and plain below, as if a voice had uttered them, were the words.

Lord keep my Memory green.

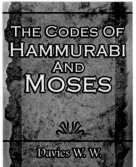

The Codes Of Hammurabi And Moses
W. W. Davies

QTY

The discovery of the Hammurabi Code is one of the greatest achievements of archaeology, and is of paramount interest, not only to the student of the Bible, but also to all those interested in ancient history...

Religion   ISBN: *1-59462-338-4*   **Pages:132**

MSRP $12.95

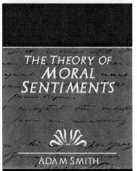

The Theory of Moral Sentiments
Adam Smith

QTY

This work from 1749. contains original theories of conscience amd moral judgment and it is the foundation for systemof morals.

Philosophy ISBN: *1-59462-777-0*   **Pages:536**

MSRP $19.95

Jessica's First Prayer
Hesba Stretton

QTY

In a screened and secluded corner of one of the many railway-bridges which span the streets of London there could be seen a few years ago, from five o'clock every morning until half past eight, a tidily set-out coffee-stall, consisting of a trestle and board, upon which stood two large tin cans, with a small fire of charcoal burning under each so as to keep the coffee boiling during the early hours of the morning when the work-people were thronging into the city on their way to their daily toil...

Pages:84

Childrens   ISBN: *1-59462-373-2*   *MSRP $9.95*

My Life and Work
Henry Ford

QTY

Henry Ford revolutionized the world with his implementation of mass production for the Model T automobile. Gain valuable business insight into his life and work with his own auto-biography... "We have only started on our development of our country we have not as yet, with all our talk of wonderful progress, done more than scratch the surface. The progress has been wonderful enough but..."

Pages:300

Biographies/ ISBN: *1-59462-198-5*   *MSRP $21.95*

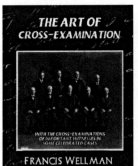

The Art of Cross-Examination
Francis Wellman

QTY

I presume it is the experience of every author, after his first book is published upon an important subject, to be almost overwhelmed with a wealth of ideas and illustrations which could readily have been included in his book, and which to his own mind, at least, seem to make a second edition inevitable. Such certainly was the case with me; and when the first edition had reached its sixth impression in five months, I rejoiced to learn that it seemed to my publishers that the book had met with a sufficiently favorable reception to justify a second and considerably enlarged edition. ...

Pages:412

Reference   ISBN: *1-59462-647-2*   *MSRP $19.95*

On the Duty of Civil Disobedience
Henry David Thoreau

QTY

Thoreau wrote his famous essay, On the Duty of Civil Disobedience, as a protest against an unjust but popular war and the immoral but popular institution of slave-owning. He did more than write—he declined to pay his taxes, and was hauled off to gaol in consequence. Who can say how much this refusal of his hastened the end of the war and of slavery ?

Law   ISBN: *1-59462-747-9*   **Pages:48**
                                             MSRP $7.45

Dream Psychology Psychoanalysis for Beginners
Sigmund Freud

QTY

Sigmund Freud, born Sigismund Schlomo Freud (May 6, 1856 - September 23, 1939), was a Jewish-Austrian neurologist and psychiatrist who co-founded the psychoanalytic school of psychology. Freud is best known for his theories of the unconscious mind, especially involving the mechanism of repression; his redefinition of sexual desire as mobile and directed towards a wide variety of objects; and his therapeutic techniques, especially his understanding of transference in the therapeutic relationship and the presumed value of dreams as sources of insight into unconscious desires.

Pages:196

Psychology   ISBN: *1-59462-905-6*   *MSRP $15.45*

The Miracle of Right Thought
Orison Swett Marden

QTY

Believe with all of your heart that you will do what you were made to do. When the mind has once formed the habit of holding cheerful, happy, prosperous pictures, it will not be easy to form the opposite habit. It does not matter how improbable or how far away this realization may see, or how dark the prospects may be, if we visualize them as best we can, as vividly as possible, hold tenaciously to them and vigorously struggle to attain them, they will gradually become actualized, realized in the life. But a desire, a longing without endeavor, a yearning abandoned or held indifferently will vanish without realization.

Pages:360

Self Help   ISBN: *1-59462-644-8*   *MSRP $25.45*

www.bookjungle.com *email: sales@bookjungle.com fax: 630-214-0564 mail: Book Jungle PO Box 2226 Champaign, IL 61825*

QTY

The Rosicrucian Cosmo-Conception Mystic Christianity *by Max Heindel* ISBN: *1-59462-188-8* **$38.95**
The Rosicrucian Cosmo-conception is not dogmatic, neither does it appeal to any other authority than the reason of the student. It is: not controversial, but is: sent forth in the, hope that it may help to clear... New Age/Religion Pages 646

Abandonment To Divine Providence *by Jean-Pierre de Caussade* ISBN: *1-59462-228-0* **$25.95**
"The Rev. Jean Pierre de Caussade was one of the most remarkable spiritual writers of the Society of Jesus in France in the 18th Century. His death took place at Toulouse in 1751. His works have gone through many editions and have been republished... Inspirational/Religion Pages 400

Mental Chemistry *by Charles Haanel* ISBN: *1-59462-192-6* **$23.95**
Mental Chemistry allows the change of material conditions by combining and appropriately utilizing the power of the mind. Much like applied chemistry creates something new and unique out of careful combinations of chemicals the mastery of mental chemistry... New Age Pages 354

The Letters of Robert Browning and Elizabeth Barret Barrett 1845-1846 vol II ISBN: *1-59462-193-4* **$35.95**
by Robert Browning and Elizabeth Barrett Biographies Pages 596

Gleanings In Genesis (volume I) *by Arthur W. Pink* ISBN: *1-59462-130-6* **$27.45**
Appropriately has Genesis been termed "the seed plot of the Bible" for in it we have, in germ form, almost all of the great doctrines which are afterwards fully developed in the books of Scripture which follow... Religion/Inspirational Pages 420

The Master Key *by L. W. de Laurence* ISBN: *1-59462-001-6* **$30.95**
In no branch of human knowledge has there been a more lively increase of the spirit of research during the past few years than in the study of Psychology, Concentration and Mental Discipline. The requests for authentic lessons in Thought Control, Mental Discipline and... New Age Business Pages 422

The Lesser Key Of Solomon Goetia *by L. W. de Laurence* ISBN: *1-59462-092-X* **$9.95**
This translation of the first book of the "Lernegton" which is now for the first time made accessible to students of Talismanic Magic was done, after careful collation and edition, from numerous Ancient Manuscripts in Hebrew, Latin, and French... New Age Occult Pages 92

Rubaiyat Of Omar Khayyam *by Edward Fitzgerald* ISBN:*1-59462-332-5* **$13.95**
Edward Fitzgerald, whom the world has already learned, in spite of his own efforts to remain within the shadow of anonymity, to look upon as one of the rarest poets of the century, was born at Bredfield, in Suffolk, on the 31st of March, 1809. He was the third son of John Purcell... Music Pages 172

Ancient Law *by Henry Maine* ISBN: *1-59462-128-4* **$29.95**
The chief object of the following pages is to indicate some of the earliest ideas of mankind, as they are reflected in Ancient Law, and to point out the relation of those ideas to modern thought. Religion History Pages 452

Far-Away Stories *by William J. Locke* ISBN: *1-59462-129-2* **$19.45**
"Good wine needs no bush, but a collection of mixed vintages does. And this book is just such a collection. Some of the stories I do not want to remain buried for ever in the museum files of dead magazine-numbers an author's not unpardonable vanity..." Fiction Pages 272

Life of David Crockett *by David Crockett* ISBN: *1-59462-250-7* **$27.45**
"Colonel David Crockett was one of the most remarkable men of the times in which he lived. Born in humble life, but gifted with a strong will, an indomitable courage, and unremitting perseverance... Biographies/New Age Pages 424

Lip-Reading *by Edward Nitchie* ISBN: *1-59462-206-X* **$25.95**
Edward B. Nitchie, founder of the New York School for the Hard of Hearing, now the Nitchie School of Lip-Reading, Inc, wrote "LIP-READING Principles and Practice". The development and perfecting of this meritorious work on lip-reading was an undertaking... How-to Pages 400

A Handbook of Suggestive Therapeutics, Applied Hypnotism, Psychic Science ISBN: *1-59462-214-0* **$24.95**
by Henry Munro Health New Age/Health/Self-help Pages 376

A Doll's House: and Two Other Plays *by Henrik Ibsen* ISBN: *1-59462-112-8* **$19.95**
Henrik Ibsen created this classic when in revolutionary 1848 Rome. Introducing some striking concepts in playwriting for the realist genre, this play has been studied the world over. Fiction/Classics/Plays 308

The Light of Asia *by sir Edwin Arnold* ISBN: *1-59462-204-3* **$13.95**
In this poetic masterpiece, Edwin Arnold describes the life and teachings of Buddha. The man who was to become known as Buddha to the world was born as Prince Gautama of India but he rejected the worldly riches and abandoned the reigns of power when... Religion History/Biographies Pages 170

The Complete Works of Guy de Maupassant *by Guy de Maupassant* ISBN: *1-59462-157-8* **$16.95**
"For days and days, nights and nights, I had dreamed of that first kiss which was to consecrate our engagement, and I knew not on what spot I should put my lips..." Fiction/Classics Pages 240

The Art of Cross-Examination *by Francis L. Wellman* ISBN: *1-59462-309-0* **$26.95**
Written by a renowned trial lawyer, Wellman imparts his experience and uses case studies to explain how to use psychology to extract desired information through questioning. How-to Science Reference Pages 408

Answered or Unanswered? *by Louisa Vaughan* ISBN: *1-59462-248-5* **$10.95**
Miracles of Faith in China Religion Pages 112

The Edinburgh Lectures on Mental Science (1909) *by Thomas* ISBN: *1-59462-008-3* **$11.95**
This book contains the substance of a course of lectures recently given by the writer in the Queen Street Hall, Edinburgh. Its purpose is to indicate the Natural Principles governing the relation between Mental Action and Material Conditions... New Age/Psychology Pages 148

Ayesha *by H. Rider Haggard* ISBN: *1-59462-301-5* **$24.95**
Verily and indeed it is the unexpected that happens! Probably if there was one person upon the earth from whom the Editor of this, and of a certain previous history, did not expect to hear again... Classics Pages 380

Ayala's Angel *by Anthony Trollope* ISBN: *1-59462-352-X* **$29.95**
The two girls were both pretty, but Lucy who was twenty-one who supposed to be simple and comparatively unattractive, whereas Ayala was credited, as her Bombwhat romantic name might show, with poetic charm and a taste for romance. Ayala when her father died was nineteen... Fiction Pages 484

The American Commonwealth *by James Bryce* ISBN: *1-59462-286-8* **$34.45**
An interpretation of American democratic political theory. It examines political mechanics and society from the perspective of Scotsman James Bryce Politics Pages 572

Stories of the Pilgrims *by Margaret P. Pumphrey* ISBN: *1-59462-116-0* **$17.95**
This book explores pilgrims religious oppression in England as well as their escape to Holland and eventual crossing to America on the Mayflower, and their early days in New England... History Pages 268

www.bookjungle.com *email: sales@bookjungle.com fax: 630-214-0564 mail: Book Jungle PO Box 2226 Champaign, IL 61825*

QTY

The Fasting Cure *by Sinclair Upton*   ISBN: *1-59462-222-1*   **$13.95**
In the Cosmopolitan Magazine for May, 1910, and in the Contemporary Review (London) for April, 1910, I published an article dealing with my experiences in fasting. I have written a great many magazine articles, but never one which attracted so much attention... New Age/Self Help Health Pages 164

Hebrew Astrology *by Sepharial*   ISBN: *1-59462-308-2*   **$13.45**
In these days of advanced thinking it is a matter of common observation that we have left many of the old landmarks behind and that we are now pressing forward to greater heights and to a wider horizon than that which represented the mind-content of our progenitors... Astrology Pages 144

Thought Vibration or The Law of Attraction in the Thought World   ISBN: *1-59462-127-6*   **$12.95**

by William Walker Atkinson   Psychology/Religion Pages 144

Optimism *by Helen Keller*   ISBN: *1-59462-108-X*   **$15.95**
Helen Keller was blind, deaf, and mute since 19 months old, yet famously learned how to overcome these handicaps, communicate with the world, and spread her lectures promoting optimism. An inspiring read for everyone... Biographies/Inspirational Pages 84

Sara Crewe *by Frances Burnett*   ISBN: *1-59462-360-0*   **$9.45**
In the first place, Miss Minchin lived in London. Her home was a large, dull, tall one, in a large, dull square, where all the houses were alike, and all the sparrows were alike, and where all the door-knockers made the same heavy sound... Childrens/Classic Pages 88

The Autobiography of Benjamin Franklin *by Benjamin Franklin*   ISBN: *1-59462-135-7*   **$24.95**
The Autobiography of Benjamin Franklin has probably been more extensively read than any other American historical work, and no other book of its kind has had such ups and downs of fortune. Franklin lived for many years in England, where he was agent... Biographies/History Pages 332

Name	
Email	
Telephone	
Address	
City, State ZIP	

☐ **Credit Card**   ☐ **Check / Money Order**

Credit Card Number	
Expiration Date	
Signature	

Please Mail to: Book Jungle
PO Box 2226
Champaign, IL 61825
or Fax to: 630-214-0564

ORDERING INFORMATION

web: *www.bookjungle.com*
email: *sales@bookjungle.com*
fax: *630-214-0564*
mail: *Book Jungle PO Box 2226 Champaign, IL 61825*
or PayPal *to sales@bookjungle.com*

Please contact us for bulk discounts

DIRECT-ORDER TERMS

**20% Discount if You Order
Two or More Books**
Free Domestic Shipping!
Accepted: Master Card, Visa,
Discover, American Express

Lightning Source UK Ltd.
Milton Keynes UK
23 December 2009

147866UK00001B/240/P